T0161250

ISLE OF THE DEAD

Originally published in German as *Toteninsel* by Zytglogge Verlag Bern, 1979
Copyright © 1979 by Zytglogge Verlag Bern
Translation and introduction copyright © 2011 by Burton Pike

First Edition, 2011

Library of Congress Cataloging-in-Publication Data

Meier, Gerhard, 1917-2008.
[Toteninsel. English]
Isle of the dead / Gerhard Meier ; translated and with an introduction by Burton Pike. -- 1st ed.
p. cm.
Originally published in German as Toteninsel in 1979.
ISBN 978-1-56478-685-2 (hbk. : alk. paper)
1. Mortality--Fiction. I. Pike, Burton. II. Title.
PT2673.E47T6713 2011
833'.914--dc22
                    2011022914

Partially funded by a grant from the Illinois Arts Council, a state agency, and by the University of Illinois at Urbana-Champaign

The publication of this work was supported by a grant from Pro Helvetia, Swiss Arts Council

The publication of this work has been supported by the Max Geilinger-Stiftung, founded in 1962 in Zurich, Switzerland, to promote the literary and cultural relations between Switzerland and the English-speaking world

www.dalkeyarchive.com

Cover: design and composition by Danielle Dutton, illustration by Nicholas Motte
Printed on permanent/durable acid-free paper and bound in the United States of America

ISLE OF THE DEAD
A NOVEL BY GERHARD MEIER

TRANSLATED AND WITH AN INTRODUCTION
BY BURTON PIKE

DALKEY ARCHIVE PRESS
CHAMPAIGN · DUBLIN · LONDON

INTRODUCTION

Two elderly friends are strolling through the Swiss city of Olten on November 11, 1977, St. Martin's Day. As they dodge cars, trucks, traffic, and weave their way through the urban life around them, the expansive principal talker, Baur, reminisces about his childhood in the small town of Amrain, his family, and his experiences to his mostly silent, recessive friend Bindschädler. Bindschädler replies sparsely and obliquely, or simply records his thoughts and observations. The reader might be tempted to consider them as two aspects of the same character.

This novel, *Toteninsel*—the title is that of Arnold Böcklin's famous painting—was published in 1979 as the first part of a tetralogy, which also includes *Borodino* (1982), *Die Ballade vom Schneien* (The Ballad of Snowing, 1985) and *Land der Winde* (Land of the Winds, 1990). The tone of *Island of the Dead* is elegiac and the setting autumnal, the dead and the past itself coming vibrantly alive only in Baur's recollections of his earlier life. Early November is the time for remembering the dead, and the novel is perfused with a sense of the transience of human life, insistently present in the wind that almost seems one of the novel's characters. Death is presented as at best a return of the elements of the body to the grass and flowers as part of the great cycle of nature, which is celebrated throughout the book.

Island of the Dead is a subtle novel about a meticulously detailed world. What distinguishes it from other modern novels, from the works of Robert Walser and Thomas Bernhard for instance, is that it is written from the heart; it does not convey an alienation from life but a sense of wonder, expressed with wit and humor, and beneath the wonder, regret.

This book is deeply autobiographical. Its author has said that the fictional Amrain is the "alias" for the small Swiss town of Niederbipp, where he was born and grew up and where he deliberately chose to live all his life, in spite of his acquaintance with the wider world, and even though he liked to travel and in his later years achieved considerable recognition for his writing.

It is its style, its progression of spiraling sentences, which carries the structural weight of *Island of the Dead*. The reader is alerted to this by the novel's epigraph, a quotation from Flaubert: "What I find beautiful, and would like to do, is a book about nothing." (Flaubert went on to add: "a book . . . that would be held together by the internal force of its style.") Proust, who also lurks in the background, is just one of many writers, books, painters, paintings, composers, pieces of music, films, and filmmakers who are specifically mentioned or alluded to in Meier's tetralogy. But the nineteenth-century Austrian novelist Adalbert Stifter seems especially important to an understanding of Meier's style. Stifter is mentioned by name several times; Bindschädler gave Baur Stifter's works, but doesn't know whether Baur ever read them. The title of Stifter's most famous novel, *Nachsommer* (*Indian Summer*), occurs frequently, usually in connection with this novel's November season, but always with a hovering echo of the Austrian writer. Stifter believed that the true markers of human life and destiny are to be found in the slow processes of nature, not the dramatic ones, and that it is the random events of daily life that constitute its essence. Stifter called this the "gentle law" of life. The characters' stroll through Olten is just such a sequence, and the revivified past of Amrain a whole series of them. Stifter is also echoed when Meier's character Baur describes his longing to become a writer: "'Bindschädler, I've thought a whole life long of writing.—Without wanting to torture you now with my views on literature, I still must say that for me a novel can be compared to a carpet, a hand-woven carpet, in creating which special attention is paid to the colors and motifs, which repeat themselves, varied of course, hand-made, marked almost by a certain ponderousness, and which remind one of a girl from school days and a field of flowers with cherry trees in it that are just blossoming; one would like to be walking across this field of flowers at least once more, and of course not alone.'"

In another place Baur says about the small town of Amrain, the emotional center of the novel: "'Bindschädler, Amrain is a carpet, if not a Persian one still a carpet with motifs. The motifs are the generations, the clans, the families. The warp is the landscape, the woof is time. Some of the motifs are fresh and shining, others appear somewhat worn, still others threadbare, and furthermore there are places where only the warp is visible.'"

But there is a Proustian disjunction between the past and present times of the novel. The daily experience Baur recounts is recollected experience; the up-to-date world of the city of Olten in which they are strolling is directly observed in Bindschädler's cool, meticulous descriptions of its natural and contemporary features. The city's bustle constantly intrudes on their walk, but is cacophonous and humanly empty: Olten is a real place of mapped streets and traffic, the world of nature confined to its parks, its chaotic department store featuring artificial flowers. Baur and Bindschädler enjoy their stroll through the city and certain of its sights, but it is the world of the imagination, not the city, that furnishes the threads that can be woven into a work of art, Baur's novel as a carpet. The startling final statement in the novel puts Meier's credo into stark relief, and explains why what overarches both the recollected and the present worlds in this book is the impersonality of time passing, of how things that present themselves as fixed change inexorably. (The epigraph to the third novel in the series, *Die Ballade vom Schneien*, is from Proust: "The only true paradises are the paradises one has lost.")

Constant here are the insistent wind, the drifting clouds, the autumnal leaf-whirling and coat-billowing gusts and breezes, and the ever-recurring cycle of nature. The reader should relax into the aura of the characters' thoughts and observations, and over the first few pages let himself or herself be drawn into the absorbing world that Meier has so skillfully created.

I would like to thank Tamara S. Evans, who introduced me to Meier's work and helped me with many of his difficult Swiss expressions; Peter Constantine, who encouraged me and made many valuable suggestions; and Catherine Scharf, Consul and Head of the Cultural Department of the Consulate General of Switzerland in New York, who kindly lent me the DVD of a 2007 documentary film on Meier by Friedrich Kappeler, *Das Wolkenschattenboot* (The Boat of Cloud Shadows).

BURTON PIKE

2011

"What seems to me beautiful and
what I would like to do is a book about nothing."
—GUSTAVE FLAUBERT

ISLE OF THE DEAD

"Bindschädler, at three, four, five one lives off the images, the thoughts one has inherited, as a dowry for life.—At sixty-three, -four, -five one walks along a river of a Saturday, declares it North American, feels its gray, orange, yellow tones as Indian tones, hallucinates a canoe on it, with the last Mohican inside, crowned with two, three colorful feathers. And one understands, glancing at the oaks by the river, that the Germanic tribes revered oaks. And one looks back on the decades of duties fulfilled as a citizen," Baur stumbled, "that is, on decades when one produced shoes for example, rifles, made bricks, tiles, bicycles, cars, television sets, and so forth, or made oneself useful in some other way, focusing on punctually observing the start of the workday, the end of the workday, above all the start. And one remembers having tried to keep body and limbs clean all those years, the dirtying oneself that comes from inside and that comes from outside, from the street for example, from the lathe, from jam, to get rid of it, also the dirt between the toes and other parts. And you think of the Eau de Cologne you poured in your left hand to spread on your cheeks, neck, nape, forehead. And you think of the Eau de Cologne you poured in your right hand to spread on your cheeks, neck, nape, forehead. You see again the clothes that you put on, all those years; you see particularly the pants, and of these especially the legs, which couldn't be too long or too wide; but the jackets had to meet certain requirements too, for instance they absolutely had to have two and not three buttons in front, had to provide as it were freedom in the elbows, had to provide as far as possible pockets with flaps; coats likewise, coats in gabardine or in herringbone pattern; and umbrellas too surge into memory (the most recent ones springing open automatically)—and hats, berets, and above all of course shoes, which fascinated one again and again by their smell, their color (especially chestnut brown), their form—all that is really quite clear. And you think of the relations you entered into with the tender sex, that is, with a quite specific representative of this tender sex. And one is surprised that a tie of this kind can endure over decades, which would be impossible to ascribe to one's own merits (and that "with the tender sex" is of course farcical). And one sees before one the children who issued from this connection, the son for example, as a three-, four-, five-year-old boy in late summer, Indian summer, or autumn, and how delighted he is with rolling potatoes, piling them in a heap as if he were counting them; or one sees one of the daughters as a three-, four-, five-year-old girl digging up wild carrots on the embankment of the local Amrain railroad, between the tracks, from which she could only be coaxed away by the threats of her playmates to call the police," Baur said, stopped, looked at three gulls flying up the river, more or less at the height of the oaks, setting down, letting themselves drift, endeavoring to keep facing upriver.

"One remembers all that, Bindschädler, not to speak of the orgasms that crown life like the feathers on the head of the last

Mohican," Baur said, lifting his left heel (in place), setting it down, lifting it, and so on, with an expression that indicated a concentration of the senses.

Rail cars coupled, far off. On the river the gulls floated past. A gust of wind brought exhaust fumes. We walked on.

"We were cleaning up the borders," Baur said, "because we wanted to put down composted soil. The trees, at least those that still had leaves, most of their leaves, stood there like torches, above all, of course, the cherry and the pear trees. It was almost evening. At times the leaves of the cherry trees vibrated as if on command, only to expire as one into a kind of immobility. And you know, Bindschädler, I am a visual person: the trunks and branches of the cherry trees, especially the trunks, were black, making the cherry trees seem like torches on black posts, occasionally flown over or even swarmed around by crows, although to point out the crows' blackness here would be unnecessarily specific, for crows simply are black. But when they, the crows, appear too often and in unusual numbers I feel somewhat uneasy, because crows seem at times to be accompanied by imminent misfortune, which of course almost borders on superstition, crows and misfortune.

"So when my wife and I were recently working in the garden and heard voices from the east side of the house, one still had something like Chopin *Etudes* in one's head, for that odd behavior of the leaves evoked piano music, and why not then music of Chopin, for it seems really saturated with Polish, Galician autumns, with torches on black posts, whose wraps, who knows for what reason, tremble at times, only to again motionlessly enclose a light around which crows are swarming. So one heard voices from the east side of the house, walked toward them, and was abruptly standing before three women, women with winter asters, whose bouquets were so large that they were forced to carry them in their arms, which led one to see godmothers in these three women, with children to be baptized in or on their arms, bedded in pastel-colored winter asters, which in turn conjured up a correspondence in art, Picasso's *Woman with Rooster*, in my opinion his most beautiful painting, although you feel that this 'most beautiful' is misplaced, for superlative sloganistic gestures really do consort badly with decent, serious consideration of paintings, texts, or musical performances," Baur said, with an expression as if he were trying to make out sounds of some kind.

A light plane circled over the town, came in for a landing on the small airfield nearby. The housefronts on the opposite riverbank appeared classical or bore traits of art nouveau, or the simple lines of our own day.

"What distinguished the three women with winter asters from real godmothers was their clothing: two were wearing black coats, one just a jacket. In addition, all three were quite old: my three sisters, named Julia, Gisela, Johanna. Julia was the one with the jacket. Greetings were exchanged, the three sisters invited into the house, their parental house, Gisela and Johanna were urged to take off their coats, and sat down around the table.

"Gisela and Johanna related that in Zurich they had visited the graves of Hans, Benno, Niklaus, Karl, and Ludwig, had traveled yesterday to Werdenburg to visit Ferdinand's grave (the grave of Gisela's husband), and now today they had come to Amrain to go together with Julia to the Amrain cemetery, where they had planted a sprig of erica among the pansies on the freshly planted grave of their mother, which of course represented a certain intrusion in the new plantings, for which they begged forgiveness.

"According to the numbers on the stone it had been determined that Mother had been born over a hundred years ago, on the island of Rügen (which made me think of Caspar David Friedrich, my mother, and blossoming alfalfa together, although I don't know if that's right about the blossoming alfalfa, but I've never been on the island of Rügen, so I could not have seen any blossoming alfalfa there, which on the other hand doesn't justify my corrective intervention in this image), where the three of them, Gisela, Julia, Johanna, and also brother Benno likewise were born, and it had been ascertained with painful surprise and displeasure that our father's grave had been leveled, as had sister-in-law Lina's, the first wife of Philipp, the second-oldest brother, although their bones were still lying in the same place, at least for the time being; just that now grass was growing over them, there were no longer any gravestones, any flowers; and they had visited the newly built mortuary, which had robbed the cemetery of its village character. Missing above all was also the elm that had certainly shaded the graves for hundreds of years while winter's harsh hoarfrost transformed its top into antlers belonging to a being that was awaiting the awakening of those who were eternally slumbering, in order to escort them there where there are no shadows, no winter; all of this reminding one of the reproductions that earlier adorned bedroom walls and that depicted the Isle of the Dead, which didn't mean that she, Johanna, particularly cared for those reproductions, upon which Gisela said Ferdinand's tombstone was wonderfully preserved, showing no signs of moss or lichen. She had to confess that unfortunately one no longer knew what sort of stone Ferdinand's tombstone was. It came out that it was of black marble, which in turn led one to understand that, in contrast to limestone, Jurassic stone, no lichen or moss could thrive on it (on highly polished marble, that is). That induced me to object that I found the patina of moss and lichens beautiful, which unleashed an energetic rebuttal and the demand that I go wash Mother's tombstone for once.

"Bindschädler, several of our other relatives are also buried in the cemetery of Amrain, the Bergers for example, one of whom spent his life trying to get hold of an inheritance from England, so it was only as a sideline that he worked in an iron factory and as a small farmer. My cousin Albert Baur lies there too, a clockmaker by profession, clockmaker all his life; he had a stiff, shorter leg, a special bicycle, usually the stump of a cigar in his mouth, something like roguishness in his eyes, and on my only visit showed me his workshop, which was lodged in a large attic whose walls were filled with ticking clocks. Cousin Albert died when the horse chestnuts were falling. Later, after his wife had died too, a preacher took over the property, removed the nameplate above the entrance, an enamel nameplate on which was written black on white *Albert Baur/Clockmaker*, and painted the house, painting over the inscription prominently displayed on the south side that likewise proclaimed *Albert Baur/Clockmaker*, but which could only be read by few people, by a few churchgoers for example, who took the little alley by the church on their way home, or by the few neighbors who knew him, Albert Baur, clockmaker, anyway. Now the housefront is on the south side, facing open ground, painted gray, clean and unwritten on," Baur said, reaching for the leaf of a shrub while walking, and plucking it so that the affected twig snapped back violently and the leaf in Baur's hand twisted around its own axis, now to the right, now to the left.

"I can," Baur said, "hardly imagine my oldest sister, Gisela, without at the same time conjuring up the image of her husband Ferdinand, who, when they both came to Amrain on a visit, went behind the house and facing the cherry tree said: 'I don't let any of my cherry trees get so tall. I saw them all off on top. I don't want any more tall cherry trees.' This cherry tree, Bindschädler, is still standing today. Every so often one saws off its dead branches to keep the tree from dying too quickly. The bark of the trunk is badly furrowed, but is regularly checked for harmful insects by a woodpecker, which pecks the bark in reverse, hopping from top to bottom, always listening, the hammering of its beak so violent that one worries about the gray matter in the woodpecker's brain.

"Bindschädler, whenever I chance to look at the cherry tree it can happen that brother-in-law Ferdinand says: 'I don't let any of my cherry trees get so tall. I saw them all off on top. I don't want any more tall cherry trees.' Which presumably sounds from that realm where there are no shadows, no winter (freely after Johanna).

"We drank tea, my three sisters (who had deposited their bouquets on a bench), my wife, and I. And one said to oneself, anyway it is the time of the dead, strictly speaking it was the first and second of November, when one particularly remembers the dead, visits them in the cemeteries, that is their graves, adorns them, even places a bowl of rice on them, or sometimes it's only pasta, and in many places one puts candles on them, or the women sit on the graves. Gisela said she had always tried, as they knew, to have Benno lie by the wall, and he had to be crowded in. At that time the new cemetery wasn't ready, so that in the old one the dead had to be placed as close to each other as possible. That brought brother Benno to my mind, laid out in the aforementioned cemetery, but as a young man, as I knew him from photos, the sport ribbon across his chest, decorated with two, three medals. Then the sports certificate intruded, which months before had turned up by accident among all the rubbish and that he, Benno, must have sported home pretty precisely a year before I was born and that since then had lain around our family seat, where I, as mentioned, had begun a year later to puff, scream, crap, drink (sharing the maternal milk, incidentally, with a notary's daughter, a girl from Amrain)," Baur said.

The tires of an automobile screeched. A car backing up stopped. The driver of the screeching car twisted his left index finger on his left temple. There was a smell of gasoline.

"Why, Bindschädler, when one is old, does one have this crazy need—to look backward or to live with our yesterdays, or to grasp again and again the threads that bind one with what has passed away, vanished, is irretrievable, that must somewhere have dissolved and yet is present, not to be got rid of? That is then somehow laid with us in the earth, where it dissolves or would have to pass along into the mineral, the material, in order to become present above us in flowers, lilies for example, asters, snowdrops, forget-me-nots, as their aroma (insofar as they are pleased to dispense such)," Baur said.

Through the nearly bare trees one could observe the quietly flowing Aare, its colorations, which it had taken from the colorations of its banks, but also from those of the sky.

"Are the plastic flowers," Baur said, "the plastic flowers that appear increasingly on our graves a sign that we increasingly take less and less with us into our graves, less and less of what has passed away, vanished, is irretrievable, that then passes into the lilies over us, into the forget-me-nots, the snowdrops, and that streams out as their fragrance (insofar as they are pleased to dispense such). Upon which this aroma can in turn produce in those left behind this crazy need—to look backward or to live with our yesterdays. So it can just keep going around and around, Bindschädler. Concerning which, the plastic flowers can of course have something quite special about them, something almost able to signal a new epoch, an epoch attempting to enter into competition with nature in a painfully awkward way, and in which these competing products, the plastic lilies for example, derisively outlast the genuine products, the *ordinary* lilies for example, many times over." Baur reached out for a chestnut leaf. "So that something painful attaches to the plastic flowers in that they exhibit the awkwardly moving quality that characterizes shoddy things, especially plastic bouquets," Baur said, stroking at the same time with the back of his left hand over the poster PATRIA / YOUR SECURITY / 99 YEARS PATRIA / FOR ALL YOUR INSURANCE PROTECTION on a wall of posters on the Gösgerstrasse.

"Bindschädler, now and then, mornings, I walk through town to buy bread at the far end, in the bakery where my girlfriend from school Linda grew up. Today this establishment still belongs to Linda, but she doesn't live in Amrain any more. Linda's father too was a gymnast, even won prizes. I believe he wore a double prize sash when he marched off to festive occasions of the gymnastics club.

"Whenever I approach Linda's establishment, Bindschädler, I ask myself: 'Did the baker, Linda's father, really enter through these doors, occasionally crowned with a wreath of laurel, the double prize sash across his chest?' And whenever the baker marched off to festive gymnastic occasions he must have left through these doors, must have strode across this terrace, which still shows the same cracks, for they must be old. And the baker must have glanced over at the pergola, which is overgrown with very old wisteria that shades the two windows of the bakehouse in which Linda and I said farewell about forty-five years ago, so that after leaving school we could set out to learn to be afraid. Bindschädler, I can still today feel Linda's damp cheeks. While at school I didn't dare enter this shop, because I was afraid that the baker knew of our love.

"Sometimes, Binschädler, I can stand around in this shop, which today is twice the size it was in Linda's time, and because for example the leather worker from next door is buying bread and wine, and then, because he doesn't see well, he lays a handful of change on the counter, then another and yet another, while puffing on his pipe, down which spittle drips, occasionally gathering into drops on the pipe bowl and hanging there a while, growing longer, slowly separating from it to fall, soundlessly of course, but its fall must still occasion a muffled, even if low, noise on the floor across which Linda walked as a child, and today, surely, still walks across at times. And I look at the door leading into the entrance hall, beyond which is the room that serves as a passageway to the bakehouse.

"Earlier a reddish light shimmered through the heavy drapes of this room, presumably coming from a red lampshade. Bindschädler, whenever I see this light before me it is always snowing— softly (as if it could already also have snowed loudly) and Christmas is around the corner, and a handbreadth of snow is lying on the branches of the wisteria.

"But the doors leading to the entrance hall beyond which this room lies, which in Linda's time served as the living room, must still be the same, judging by the badly worn latch whose sagging support (or whatever one wants to call it) is worn down at least a centimeter. Another time the baker's boy, hanging onto the latch, swung himself into the shop, into the entrance hall, into the . . . and so forth.

"Diagonally opposite, on the other side of the main street, lies the butcher's shop, which has been run since by various butchers and in which up until a few years ago one of those marvelous butcher's tables stood, crafted in marble and gold, that is, at least the year (in this case 1904) was displayed in gold, and in the shop likewise a few things have remained unchanged, the doors for example, the display window (outside which it has also snowed several times since), the wood-paneled ceiling (painted white), several meat hooks. The baker and butcher families back then had probably not liked each other very much, because I remember Linda telling me in school that a mouse's tail had been found in a sausage from the shop across the way—a real mouse's tail,"

Baur said, twisting the chestnut leaf by its stem, which made it resemble a fluttering hen, the whole image had something about it of "man with hen."

"As one approaches the bakery (at least as I do) one is facing the east side of the establishment. Earlier that was not the case, for a farmhouse had been built onto it that has in the meantime been torn down. So now the east side of Linda's establishment stands there exposed, exhibiting the outline of the torn-down house, so that one receives a dim impression of the depth, height, color, or paneling of the rooms, also their baseboards, of which some are still present, to say nothing of remains of floorboards, traces of pipes. It reminds one of *The Notebooks of Malte Laurids Brigge*, where a wall like that is also described," Baur said as he released the chestnut leaf, which fluttered after a trailer truck as we marched along beside the line that had formed behind it.

"One morning, Bindschädler, I was getting ready to go for some bread, looking forward to walking through Amrain, going by the forge whose first owner had fallen under the local train, he was a gymnast, top gymnast in Amrain, wore a double sash at gymnastic festivities, and who (in contrast to the baker) was delicate, but, as befits a smith, with a sinewy build—as I was getting ready to get some bread, I heard in the kitchen the buzzing of a blowfly, somewhat more indistinct than usual, but irritating enough. I went after the blowfly, opened the door, turned on the porch light. Involuntarily I had to think of Dámaso Alonso's blowfly, about which I had written Amanshauser the day before that Alonso had killed it so he could finish a poem, which then moved him to write a poem about the death of a blowfly. For Amanshauser had written me about a fly, a longish, transparent, light-green fly with gold-button eyes and coiled antennae that was just then drinking in front of him, hovering, and that comes into the room in autumn and stays the whole winter, but becomes so weak that he does not believe it could still have a spring.

"So the blowfly flies onto the porch, Bindschädler, against a window. Begins to wriggle. A spider comes, a little one, from the upper window frame. Spider and fly have at each other, violently, briefly. The spider withdraws, not before having wrapped up the fly. The blowfly wriggles as well as it can. Light mixes in, the clouds, the leaves. The blowfly gets more and more tangled up. Works free! Drops a few centimeters. Remains dangling. The spider is there. Wraps up the blowfly. Disappears back above. Leaves dance on the ground, in the air, vibrate on twigs. On the hillside cherry trees gleam. Farther down, pear trees. Here and there the hillside is greening. The blowfly wriggles and wrig— . . . works free! Flies to the next window. Hangs there. A spider . . . (a bigger one this time). Wriggle, wrig— . . . The spider retreats. Comes closer to the blowfly from below, from behind. Bites! The blowfly twitches. The twitching ebbs. The spider withdraws. The fly is dangling dead in the room.—Cones of light fall now on this, now on that part of the staffage. Three, four, five pear trees sparkle, phosphorize. Then some plum trees. A cherry tree. Clouds come up over the Jura mountains, parallel to them, on the westwind."

Baur bent down, undid the lace on his right shoe, reached under its tongue with his index and middle fingers, pulled it up, laced the shoe, repeated the same with his left shoe.

"Those clouds over the Jura, which were flying past at a pretty rapid pace, had pastel tones, which, however, did not appear as monochromatic surfaces. One cloud, for example, could show a pink of varying intensity, fading into alabaster tones on its peak and on its end. The whole thing looked like an unrolling abstract painting of enormous length.

"Occasionally holes appeared in the clouds, as I said, through which the sunlight flooded, as if searchlights were falling now on a group of cherry trees, now on two, three plum trees, and then lighting up a single pear tree.

"When I came back from Linda's bakery, Bindschädler, the dead blowfly was no longer dangling by its thread. The spider had taken it up above. In those days I was reading Gottfried Keller's *Green Henry*. The fate of little Meret and the last few minutes of the blowfly blended together. Little Meret's portrait, by the way, was hanging in a parsonage. She must have been a beautiful child, done up for the portrait in a green damask dress, gold chain, gold and silver sequins in her hair intertwined with silk threads, pearls. In the painting the girl was holding a child's skull and a white rose.

"I asked myself again why older literature—older art altogether—appears so noble, so masterly, thinking that a certain amount of cheating can be attributed to it. One thinks of land surveyors, who slip onto maps, that is to say the white spaces, fictive rivers, mountains, villages, plains, or tundras. On the other hand, art today occasionally resigns itself to white, or at least monochromatic, surfaces.

"Our life, Bindschädler, might be a region with rivers, mountains, villages, plains, or tundras, to say nothing of karst landscapes, ice fields, and bays beneath a midnight sun. To reach this region might always have been what people wanted. Bindschädler, when I see them swarming out on the weekend, treating themselves to red stockings, I have to think of the surveyors, including those who slip fictive rivers onto the white spaces of their maps, tundras and so forth. Others too seek to force themselves to reach where they are trying to get to, where there is no shadow, no winter, if only to hear distant sounds, of balalaikas perhaps," Baur said with a wink, turning to peruse the housefronts on the other side of the Aaare that were partially visible through the branches of the oaks, chestnuts, acacias.

"This little Meret, Bindschädler, keeps hiding from me behind the *Girl on Red Ground*. The *Girl on Red Ground* was painted by Albert Anker. The picture hangs in the museum in Solothurn, on the south wall (for the time being, at least). And if I keep looking at it, this girl too is holding a child's skull and a white rose. And this rose reveals itself as the one that fell from Lenore Beauregard and must have drifted out to sea—Theodor Storm's Lenore Beauregard." Baur was silent.

I saw him before me as *comrade in arms* from our time in the military, and how he marched before me in the single file while shooting stars fell; or I imagined him walking beside me on a night patrol across the Great Peat Plain, with villas around me, whole tracts of villas that the birch trees evoked in us, in half-sleep.

"The day after the visit of the three women with winter asters I passed by the garden from which their bouquets must have come. Here winter asters were blooming, short-stemmed, long-stemmed, pink, mauve, but also white blossoms shot through with a soft pink. They swayed, these winter asters, in a manner of speaking, from deep inside and pensively. And I thought of their transpirations, their odor, their aroma. And I compared the scent of the flowers with the odor, the transpirations, of people. And I considered it possible that the scent of the flowers corresponds to the odor of our genitals, of our emanations in general. But in the case of flowers the odors are considered scents, glorious aromas, unless it happens to be a question of winter asters. Which—rubbed between the fingers—have the odor of death about them, at least an odor that corpses are likely to give off," Baur said.

A trailer truck passed us. Across the Great Peat Plain we marched four abreast, in half-sleep, hallucinating residential areas. Shooting stars fell. It was winter.

"Bindschädler, you should have seen them, the three women with winter asters: Fellini figures. You know, Fellini selects his actors from among hundreds, among thousands if he has to. He is after faces, after bodies, through which something like the wind of the world plays." Baur stopped, looked at me, said: "Those three women with winter asters have become a painting for me, mounted on the east wall of the soul, at eye level. Around this picture it will of course always be November, even in the middle of summer. And the whistles of the local train will try to slash the picture diagonally. And the odor of Galician autumns will remain with it, to say nothing of the spectacle of crows from Galician spaces." Baur smiled, turned away, started walking again.

I observed the locomotive that stood as a monument in front of the workshops of the Swiss National Railways. As I did so three faces came into my mind, opal-colored, nuanced in their outline, their smiles (arising from differentiated embarrassments). And I noticed that all three were trying to make something out, land surveyors perhaps, red-stockinged, far back in the landscape.

"So the painting *Three Women with Winter Asters* is hanging on the east wall of the soul, at eye level, like little Meret's portrait was hanging in the parsonage or the *Girl on Red Ground* on the south wall of the museum in Solothurn," Baur said.

I conjured up Solothurn's chestnut-lined boulevards, especially those near the Baseltor, while Leninistic maxims popped into my mind: "Down with the kitchen" . . . "Away with pots and pans" . . . "The sauce boat is the enemy of the party cell" . . .

"You're a railroad man, Bindschädler, and I love the railroad. Which of course doesn't exclude your being allowed to have a certain fondness for the railroad too. The steam locomotive over there, standing as a souvenir before the workshops of the Swiss National Railways, always strikes me. And if I can, I always stop and look for the thousandth time at the body, its copper entrails (the external ones anyway), the stack, the wheels; on the one hand I feel the clumsiness of its shape, on the other I admire the art-nouveau, almost plantlike gracefulness of several parts, and discover qualities that seem to cancel each other out: girlish casualness—and then purposefulness (even if ponderous), reminiscent of Mother Courage. But each time I admire the coal tender too. For what would a steam locomotive be without a tender? And I come finally to the black of steam locomotives and usually find myself in the Wild West, in the midst of Indians, buffaloes. And from the cattle cars behind the locomotive *palefaces* are shooting like crazy at the buffaloes. And Indians on horses (armed with bows and arrows), follow the game from behind cover. And there are more and more dead buffaloes. And the *Song of Death* spreads out across the prairie. Train stations rise from its melody.

Blowflies take off from stubbled faces. One fly falls into the barrel of a revolver. The fingertip of one of the stubbled ones closes the mouth of the barrel. The stubbled one listens grinning to the buzzing of the blowfly. Giant chervil sways under the banner of the locomotive's smoke, whose black one easily became addicted to, turning up in the Wild West in the midst of Indians, buffaloes, *palefaces* shooting."

Baur kept his left hand in his pants pocket while his right swung freely. He inspected the sidewalk, which was strewn with leaves, above all those from the chestnut trees, while cars were pouring out exhaust, gulls crying, the Aare flowing stoically on its way.

"There are times, Bindschädler, when the aforementioned black of the locomotive even transports one to Siberia. You imagine yourself traveling through Russia on the trans-Siberian railroad," Baur said, once again reaching for the stem of a chestnut leaf lying on the hedge, twirling it back and forth between thumb and forefinger, simulating a fluttering hen whose comb would have to be reddening more and more.

Above Baur shooting stars began to fall. The front of the single-file column dissolved in the night. Cannon barked in the distance. Through the cannon barking angelic proverbs boomed: "The cause of the repression of woman is her exclusion from social production" . . . "The first precondition for her emancipation is the reintroduction of the entire female sex into public industry" . . .

Baur dropped the chestnut leaf. It fluttered after a Volkswagen. Other leaves did the same, to drift down shortly after, onto the street this time, where they fell under the wheels of cars.

"So one imagines oneself on the trans-Siberian railroad. You drink tea, look out into the birch forests, look across the tundras, the distances, arrive in Siberia. Twenty-one degrees below zero Celsius. Opal-colored landscape. You pass horse sleighs laden with long logs. You pass troikas. Night is falling. Beneath the moon (full moon, of course), thin clouds are scudding at a considerable pace, pulling gossamer veils of shadow across the bluish, unending surface of the snow. And far off wolves must be howling (at the full moon, of course) as the locomotive steams through the forests, across the tundras, the distances, dragging behind it a train of sounds, a train of balalaika sounds (interspersed with the mumbling of murdered millions), which cast shadows of sound up at the full moon, the scudding clouds, lacy shadows of sounds, as it were," Baur said. He stopped, with his left hand grabbed the crease of his left pant leg, pulled it up, ascertaining thereby that his shoelace had come untied. Baur dropped the pant leg, bent down, rolled the left pant leg up a little, tied his shoelace again, rolled down his trouserleg, straightened up, turned to me (staying where he was), and said:

"You see, one has such fancies in one's head and pictures on the walls of one's soul, *Three Women with Winter Asters* among others, on the east wall, at eye level, as mentioned. In that connection the painting *Three Women with Winter Asters* counts as a new acquisition, which occasions unusual interest. And when you as owner of the gallery (of fancies in one's head) observe *Three Women with Winter Asters*, especially Gisela, then brother-in-law Ferdinand whispers over one's shoulder into one's ear: 'I no longer let any of my cherry trees get so tall. I saw each one off on top.'

Bindschädler, this cherry tree is still standing today, in a pretty sorry state to be sure, because all the dead branches are sawed off to keep it from dying too quickly. So now it has a damaged shape, like those shapes that would materialize again along the trans-Siberian railroad, out of the forests, tundras, the gigantic distances in white, tinted blue in moonlit nights, covered with the shadowy veil of gossamer clouds, under a baldachin of lacy clouds of sound. And the aforementioned woodpecker hops in reverse down the cherry tree, pecking at the bark, listening, pecking . . . in a way that makes one anxious for its brain mass.

"In November, Bindschädler, there are more magpies, too. Perhaps one just sees them better in November? November is the most intense month, Bindschädler, at least for colors, movement, light; but also for despair, rapture. Occasionally, of course, it seems apathetic, this November, wraps itself up as it were in fog, sometimes for days, for weeks, so that the stone crosses in the fields are dripping, the farmsteads dozing sleepily, as if people, cattle, fields did not exist, the nut trees did not exist, the martens that push things around in attics at night banging about as if the farmsteads were haunted. Irritable dogs lie chained up. Roads squeeze around the farms, ending in gravel ditches, woods, plains, which are not recognizable as such. Letter carriers in capes deliver bills for light, water, heating oil, and *Uncle Tom's Cabin* perhaps," Baur said, swinging his arms.

Several gulls flew up the river, more or less at eye level, one of them screaming once, twice, three times.

"Bindschädler, believe me: poetry is the salt of life," Baur said. "Let happen what may—searchlights might light up cherry trees (celestial, alabaster-colored), it might snow, drip with fog . . . (By the way, Bindschädler, have you noticed too that before a storm houses turn blue, especially their white façades?) . . . And whatever happens may also be: the stomach might be seized by colic, loins might scream for a woman, loins might find fulfillment, daisies might signify that people can still have a spring, flies too, and so on. And whatever happens may also be: if poetry isn't part of it, at least a pinch, vegetative, then the *soup* has no salt.

"But I can't tell you, Bindschädler, what poetry is. I can't even tell you what salt is. And why our body is presumably predisposed to poetry, our life to poetry. Every child knows that. But one has to try to understand it, Bindschädler."

A locomotive whistled. Not a steam locomotive, of course. Again the coupling of rail cars was audible, mingled with automobile exhaust from the Gösgerstrasse and a mouldy smell rising from the banks of the Aare. Four, five gulls flew past above the Aare, the other way, while Baur jovially swung his right arm (his left hand in his pants pocket), staring silently before him. At the time, all the cars on the Gösgerstrasse were heading downtown.

I remarked to Baur that poetry was perhaps to be understood as a spider, as a spider within us, whose task would be not to catch blowflies of course, but to spin threads—connecting to things, likewise to things in rooms. And I said, as far as things go, that one had heard that when there will be a new sky and a new earth one would no longer think of the earlier things.

"In Alsace once I looked into a charnel house," Baur said, "into a stone vault, half cellar, half shed, built against a church. There the bones of generations lie: the thighbones of girls beside the thighbones of old men, pelvic bones of old women under metacarpal bones of youths, breastbones of elderly men above sacrums of elderly women.—And an old wind passes over them, something like a battlefield wind. And whereas in neighboring regions toy elephants tarry (especially Indian ones, stuffed with kapok, covered with glass beads and gold and silver sequins), looking east, and whereas, in my case at least, on the east wall the picture *Three Women with Winter Asters* is hanging, the bones lie all mixed up harmoniously, Bindschädler; the pelvic, carpal, and all the other bones, to say nothing of the skulls, which have something of the beet-shaped festival lanterns about them that children carry around during the nights of sugar-beet time." Baur was silent.

A wind rustled through the trees as well, even if it wasn't a battlefield wind, here and there detaching a leaf, which fell into the Aare, onto its bank, or the sidewalk.

I thought of crickets. That they belonged to the oldest group of animals that could communicate with each other by exchanging sounds. And that through their impressive repertory of communicating sounds, crickets and grasshoppers demonstrated a special talent. And that the various species differentiated themselves through the pitch and length of their chirping, which was as characteristic as, say, their body color. And that the insects sang with the help of instinctive rhythmic movements. Crickets, for example, produced their audible signals with their wings, by stroking the strip of small teeth on one edge of the top wing against the edge of the bottom one.

Baur, bending slightly forward, stared while walking at the asphalt, coming into my field of vision, as it were, out of the corner of my left eye, as he had when, as a soldier, he had cleaned off Bütikofer's army tunic with snow after the latter had slipped on the hillside while pulling up his pants. The fir trees of the Justis Valley, festooned with snow, reminded one of Adalbert Stifter, the silent man from Oberplan (Böhmerwald). I remembered having given Baur Stifter's works in six volumes as a Christmas present, without owning them myself.

"Bindschädler, everything is really motion," Baur said. "I believe: poetry, that's nothing. Movement is everything. Look, the great Neva has been flowing since God knows when. The Moskva, the Aare, the Rhine, they all move water (gravel too), rush over falls when these turn up. In the body blood flows, in the ocean the Gulf Stream, in the brain the stream of thoughts, while the bowels coil, the earth revolves."

Before the Trimbach Bridge we crossed the Gösgerstrasse on the zebra stripes, then the Industriestrasse, in order to proceed on the left sidewalk, passing, in doing so, the *Dampfhammer* factory complex, on the south side of which there is a square partly planted with maple trees that give the property (a hybrid of canteen, cabinet-maker's workshop, outbuilding of a Russian country estate) something like a historical backdrop. One walks past the first maple, then past all the rest, which—of smaller size and with ball-shaped tops—stand on the outer edge of the sidewalk, trees that one also sometimes sees outside cafés, noticing them especially in springtime on account of their flowers' symmetrical yellowish-red structures, which, were they beneath a sky of somewhat muted blue, would have prevailed as flowers and not like a product of art nouveau.

"And everything, Bindschädler, everything turns and turns. Now one thing is up, the other is down. And you fish in this confusion for a little point, for just a single life, in order to extract it together with other little points, other lives, the way one pulls out fish, trout for example, on a hook; of course with the result that their lives ebb away in death throes." Baur blew his nose.

"I like to walk through this part of town.—Do you see all those things over there? Discarded parts from building the railroad, presumably. And through them the sky, at times bare, overcast, putting on its stars: firefly-lights above the field full of parts. I like walking through it. And if I were a photographer, Bindschädler, these iron bones would be sold commercially so people could decorate their walls with them," Baur said, at the same time passing the back of his left hand across the fence of palings dividing the field of parts from the street, dividing it from the row of trees too, which consists (as mentioned) of maples with ball-shaped tops that reminded one of the head of the woodpecker tapping the trunk of the cherry tree, hopping in reverse from top to bottom.

Meanwhile we passed one of those creeping vines that had brought ambivalent pleasure to one as a boy smoking its tendrils, and which one recognizes from afar on account of their white gossamer.

"This field full of parts, Bindschädler, has become for me the *Field full of Bones* hanging on the west wall of the soul (opposite the *Three Women with Winter Asters*)," Baur said smiling, this time letting his wedding ring glide across the latticework, which made a noise as if a woodpecker were tapping directly on one's brain case.

I said to Baur that perhaps the soul resembled that little house on the Ulica Dabrowiecka in Warsaw that contains a collection of some seven thousand artworks, which Ludwig Zimmerer, the owner, declared a *paradisical cage*. The constant stream of new pictures compels a constantly new, technically sophisticated space-saving presentation, so that from behind and below something can still be conjured up. The intensity of the pictures, to which one cannot do justice by calling them "naïve," provides a deep and direct insight into the strange inner worlds of one's fellow humans. There is for example a work of Jozef Lurka proclaiming the Annunciation in wood, bringing out its theological boldness with simple piety, an *Eve with Trout in Paradise*, but by which Lurka did not mean to allude to the old Christian fish symbol for Christ; his intention was rather to illustrate what was paradisical about paradise: If a lion lets itself be stroked, that's nothing, but a trout?—Where since the fall of man has a trout let itself be stroked?

Through a newspaper story photos of the *paradisical cage* got around. One showed the niche above the staircase where below the radiator Lenin, the Last Supper, and the Holy Family coexisted, carved in wood. Another photo provided a glance into the living room, whose walls and ceiling were completely covered with pictures. Even the floor was covered with artworks, in three layers, hinged (according to the photo caption). Several people had also been captured in this photo. One, a well-known cultural editor, was (if one was not mistaken) staring up at a painting on the ceiling, while Zimmerer was standing beneath the clock that simulated something like cosmic time, where the darkness behind the two-paneled glass door brought to one's mind afterward his (Baur's) glowing lights that would be flickering above the *Field full of Bones*, but which here had only to shimmer intensely in a cosmic breeze that when the door was open must surely have wafted over these walls, this ceiling, this floor.

"Bindschädler, over there we have the *Nago Tower*.—With us you get sick from overeating, struggle against overweight, found clubs in order to weigh oneself publicly at stated intervals. And here, in this *Nago Tower*, energy food is produced or stored to beef up boys, to urge them on," Baur said, blinking, as if he had Swiss pines before him, on rocks in the light.

"Bindschädler, I wonder if I'll manage—to write? It is presumptuous, perhaps. Talking is altogether a presumption. One should hold it in like winter asters," Baur said, alluding to their silence in beauty; which on the other hand brought to mind their genital emanations and Baur's assumption that flowers, plants in general, might condescend to classify the excretions of cows, of people, as tasty morsels.

"So you could say—it's not motion either: it's stillness! Everything is stillness, one might say.—It's not poetry and it's not motion: it's stillness! The stillness, Bindschädler, that one finds in charnel houses, between piled-up thigh bones of old men and those of girls, between pelvic bones of boys and cheekbones of old women, between the breastbones of peasants and the collarbones of female factory workers.

"And when nothing will exist any longer, Bindschädler, when there are no longer flowers, bones, blowflies, rivers; that is, when the Aare no longer flows, the Rhine, the great Neva, the Moskva no longer flow—then everything will be still.—And the stillness will be the alpha and the omega.—Yes!"

Baur turned around toward the tower containing the matter out of which bodies are built. He blew his nose again, reached for the crease in his right pants leg, shook it, let go, walked on— swinging his arms.

We were approaching the underpass and leaving the enormous storage yard of discarded parts. A train was thundering over the underpass, and one subsequently heard it rolling across the Eisenbrücke.

"Bindschädler, then the three women with winter asters, you know, finally got up to leave: that is, it occurred to Johanna to mention that she had recently been to see Philipp. Things were going well with him. They went to eat together, in the usual place. You eat well and cheaply there. Philipp drank just one beer with his meal. And the restaurant people were extremely friendly, especially the proprietor, who even came over to the table to shake hands. Philipp then tried to let her know, to the extent that he could still make himself understood, what was behind this friendliness. A fight had broken out in the pub, and some ruffian had landed one on the proprietor. He, Philipp, had stood up, gone up to this ruffian, planted a hook to his chin, and gone back to his seat. The man was carried outside.

"All this had taken place, one can imagine the scene, in silence, at least on Philipp's side, since because of his missing larynx he could hardly make himself understood anymore, so that the whole incident must surely have had something of a scene in a silent film. But otherwise he was fine. And up there he was living on the hillside, they had built a kind of residential block, which really made no sense, building such boxes on hillsides, but nevertheless Philipp had a view of the lake. He was well settled with a widow, who was nice to him. And he had his own toilet in the basement, and a shower. He even had the use of a small workshop. Philipp had brought over his own tools. And he kept the boxes and space neat. Indeed, people in his building were in general quite friendly toward him. They were apparently aware of the burden he was under, of what Philipp had been through. He was often greeted by his first name, people said: 'Bonjour, Monsieur Philipp.'

"And then they had also gone to Jacques's grave. And it bothers Philipp a great deal even today that Jacques was killed crashing into a wall early one summer morning, for Jacques had been the only one in the family who had stood up for him after he (Philipp) had lost his voice.

"'Yes . . . there . . . I don't know why . . . but I'm always close to tears . . . when I'm here . . . and look around,' Julia said, looking around.

"Bindschädler, I believe Julia didn't comprehend that she was in her parents' house. But somehow she felt it. You know, these changes in the brain . . .

"Then the three women asked for their coats, that is, Gisela and Johanna asked for them, for Julia didn't have one. We left the house, went down the steps. The three women picked up their winter asters. They walked along the east front of the house to the street, stopped, looked at the house. Julia turned away, looking at a poplar, above which hung fleecy clouds. 'That tree is simply beautiful,' Julia said. 'What's the name of that tree?'—'It's a poplar. Yes, yes, a simply beautiful poplar,' I said.

"One accompanied Gisela, Julia, Johanna as far as the main street, in doing so measuring the path that Johanna, Julia, Gisela had walked often in their lives. Gisela's husband, brother-in-law Ferdinand, the one who didn't want any tall cherry trees, was, by the way, a cellulose cooker. He cooked trees, over the course of his life whole forests, kept a Harley-Davidson, and as a sideline several cows, a horse, two, three wagons, harvest wagons, a plow, a plow for potatoes too, a harrow, a German shepherd; planted potatoes, wheat, mangelwurzel, used these up during the winter as feed, mixed with flour, chopped straw, bran; in June turned the cut grass on the fields, together with Gisela, their three sons, after he had returned from the cellulose factory when the the early shift finished, on the Harley-Davidson, occasionally scattering hens along the road, which was still there at that time—along the road.—But for his main profession brother-in-law Ferdinand remained a cellulose cooker, cooked trees, over the course of his life whole forests, came over occasionally to Amrain, took up a position behind the house and said: 'I no longer let my cherry trees get so tall. I saw them all off on top. I don't want any more tall cherry trees.' Mondays he was again cooking wood, over the course of his life whole forests, as mentioned, also including Finnish trees that had come down Finnish rivers, then by railroad to the cellulose factory. Where they were chopped up, cooked by cellulose cooks. So brother-in-law Ferdinand had had a lot to do with wood all his life. And at the end, when in his wooden coffin he left the Harley-Davidson, wife, and family to rest in the earth, Gisela said that he was cold now, and always, whenever she looked over at the cemetery, she felt cold too. Meanwhile fir trees were being cooked in the cellulose factory, whole fir forests, so that paper would be available for newspapers, books, letters, and so forth, in order to hold on, minutely, as it were, to whatever happens day after day, although day after day the same things happen.

"So Ferdinand cooked trees—quasi as a farmer. Philipp painted houses (for a while at least)—so to speak as a boxer. In Langenthal there's a house that Philipp painted. And always when I pass it I have to think of Philipp, the boxer who painted houses. And I am overcome with pity for painters who aren't painters. And when I pass by the cemetery in Werdenburg, Bindschädler, I say to myself: 'There lies Ferdinand, freezing.' So there's always something to remember. Firs too, fir forests, occasionally remind me of Ferdinand, to say nothing of the newspapers, books, and so forth. Once, by way of exception, he showed up, brother-in-law Ferdinand, on his Harley-Davidson, organizing a motocross on the *Field full of Bones*, under the eyes of the three women with winter asters. This motocross took place in total silence, corresponding to the terrain and the *Field full of Bones*.

"Bindschädler, I believe it's not stillness either—the alpha and omega. I think it's love! Love is more than poetry, motion, stillness. And with love between the sexes it's unfulfilled love that is one's great love, a love that resembles a field of winter asters, under Galician light, surrounded by torches on black posts whose coverings seem at times to tremble, and then to motionlessly enclose a light, surrounded by a swarm of cawing crows. Yes!" Baur said, his left hand in his pants pocket, his right hand swinging. It made one shiver.

"I've strayed from the subject, Bindschädler. But our life, our thinking, is probably a constant deviation, although one doesn't really know what one is deviating from, in order finally to deviate to where there are no shadows, no winter. So, Bind-schädler, love isn't the final thing either: it's God. God, who is all in all: poetry, motion, stillness, love. And his throne is presumably in a city of spirits whose houses resembles the little house on the Ulica Dabrowiecka that contains a collection of some seven thousand artworks, whose constant increase demands a carefully thought out presentation so that from in back and below something can always be conjured up (freely after Bindschädler)," Baur said smiling, making Eve appear to stroke the trout even more energetically (at least the trout in the portrayal of *Eve with Trout in Paradise*).

Then the fir trees came to mind, bent down with snow, reminding me of Stifter, the silent man from Oberplan (Böhmer-wald), who died in Linz, not far from the monastery of St. Florian, where Anton Bruckner's sarcophagus stands, whose outer case one was allowed the privilege of touching with one's fingertips when one made the pilgrimage to Bruckner at St. Florian's, that is, to his remains in the sarcophagus. And on this occasion one perceived that monasteries shape the landscape, or the other way around perhaps, that specific landscapes might have attracted monasteries. Two, three men were just coming out of the BERNA truck factory, presumably interested customers.

"Apropos BERNA," Baur said, "that's where a neighbor of ours did his apprenticeship. Then he looked up at an odd angle, steadfastedly, and his eyes got even bluer. Now he's a teacher. Another neighbor did his apprenticeship over there, in the Swiss National Railways workshop. He later became a letter carrier, postal policeman, alongside that or in turn a local councilman, insurance agent, on the staff of a firm in Amrain that processes pig intestines. During his military service he transmitted greetings on the postal packages he sent one, which were of course met with joy every time. He acquired a family, a house, a car. He died early, of cancer. But the sour cherries on the north wall keep on ripening. Only the rabbit hutch was put to other uses. The hedge of wild roses can hardly be restrained. The birch trees must be cleared, the house painted, the road to the house paved, the business with the sewage straightened out."

The odor of tar now hung in the air. The noise of traffic made itself heard from the Gösgerstrasse, which we had again approached in a wide arc.

"The *Dampfhammer* factory over there on the Industriestrasse always reminds me of Russia, Bindschädler, brings up pictures of railroad workers on strike, gathering around them a whole section of Moscow, through whose streets icy winds blow. And the people are wearing black coats. And over the quarter lies twilight, horror. In the workshops they are working their fingers to the bone. Yes!—I love these landscapes on the edge of cities, Bindschädler, these industrial streets, even though there is something inhuman about them. And this area, as mentioned, is where two of our neighbors did their apprenticeship as fitters, one of whom became a letter carrier, postal policeman, alongside that or in turn local councilman, insurance agent, on the staff of a firm in Amrain that processes pig intestines, finally to rest in the cemetery, where he is probably freezing too," Baur said.

"And so, while my cousin Albert Baur's many clocks were ticking in his attic in cacophonous confusion, measuring time to beat the band, each clock out of vanity seizing time for itself in order to be the first, the only one, to measure it best—so while the many clocks were ticking on the four walls of my cousin's attic (who, moreover, limped because of one shorter leg, which called for a special bicycle with a shortened pedal rod, so that one leg, I think the right one, pedaled normally, the other hardly at all), my Amrain rode along, that is, it partook in the widely diffused motion of all neighboring points on the surface of the earth, rode along through space, revolved in the great revolving around the earth's axis, around the sun. And there was conception in this my Amrain, especially nights, when the breezes played around the houses, sang in the wires, the telegraph wires; it could of course also happen during the day, for example on Sundays, in the morning or after lunch. And there was dying in my Amrain. And the children went to school if they didn't happen to be on vacation. And those who couldn't yet go to school envied those who could go to school. And the children who had to go to school envied those who already had school behind them. And those who had left school lost themselves in memories of their time in school. And Father looked after the insane, brother-in-law Ferdinand cooked trees, Philipp painted housefronts, two of my cousins played trumpet, marching along four abreast, the banner in front. And clouds passed over Amrain on the west wind, east wind. Makers of radiators knocked sand into the pipes in order to bend them. The smell of meals brought from home penetrated classrooms, as did the knocking of the radiator makers. Starlings hung on the schoolroom walls, sparrows, goldfinches, swallows, crows, buzzards, owls, woodpeckers, magpies, in pictures of course. Girls pushed notes over to the boys. Out-of-season flies indulged in bouquets of daffodils, cowslips, violets that decorated the desks of the teachers. Teachers were awaiting atlases with redrawn borders. Rabbits ate dandelions." Baur stopped, stuck his hands in his pants pockets, looked over at the BERNA factory, then at the spherical tank. "A hostile area, really," Baur said.

"Bindschädler, a psychiatrist once made me a sketch of the psychiatric clinic *Burghölzli*. I never made use of it, that is, I never went there. Earlier, madhouses were often located in empty monasteries.

"I recently saw a painting of the *Rosegg* (psychiatric hospital in Solothurn), a painting by Rosa Wiggli, the mother of the iron sculptor Oscar Wiggli. Its painted walls radiated a strange light," Baur said, raising his left pant leg slightly, presumably to check whether his shoelace was tied.

"While paper was being processed from Ferdinand's cellulose, Bindschädler, paper for letters to brides, for example, here or there a clan became extinct, almost an entire people, a bird species too; meanwhile countless animal species have been able to survive through constant breeding, adaptation, countless flowers as well: nasturtiums, for example, violets, winter asters; among trees even the firs," Baur said.

I again caught myself thinking of the crickets, of how they make music by stroking the strip of small teeth on the edge of the top wing against the edge of the bottom one.

"In autumn, when the plums were picked and there were still enough blue tones present, the noise from the working of fruit-press screens began to sound over Amrain; for now the farmers were bringing their apples to the locksmith, who had a spindle press that had to be worked by hand, and finally, when the resistance was great enough, the apples could only be pressed from screen to screen, which produced those bright, metallic sounds that overspread Amrain through windless blue days whose stillness was disturbed at most by the scream of a calf, a pig, from the slaughterhouse. The meadow saffron were already past their bloom, while the dahlias looked up at the sky in painful beauty.

"The farmers' wives would plant one corner of the place set aside for plants with dahlias, so that a boquet of dahlias suddenly towered up abruptly out of the fields, as it were, and the wind could wander through them under a sky of September or October blue. In the pubs of Amrain it smelled of beer, of fortified wine. On Sundays hunters headed out for the forest to scout for wild animals, where they could be found. The bicycle clubs were making their final tours. The gymnastic clubs were holding their championships. Children were making kites. The threshers were having their high season," Baur said.

I looked at him from the side and saw him as a soldier, striding before me in an ice tunnel; imagined myself immersed in greenish light and filled with the hope of being able to look out over a late summer landscape at the end of the tunnel.

"Bindschädler, when I walk through Amrain these days on my way to the bakery, which, as I mentioned, still belongs to Linda today, although Linda no longer lives in Amrain but in the city where the *Girl on Red Ground* hangs—when I walk through the town mornings and come across the wall that preserves the cross-section of that torn-down house and resembles the wall that Rilke described in *The Notebooks of Malte Laurids Brigge*, it can happen that I am not strolling through an overcast Amrain but through a gossamer, pastel-colored painting of Joseph Mallord William Turner's in which the flowers are upside down, that is to say with their tops rooting in a Turneresque ground.

"The torn-down house belonged to a landowner who is dead. His wife is dead too. Only in the book that came out during the Second World War, *The Successful Planter*, are they still standing harmoniously together, in a blossoming field of potatoes, captioned: 'He and she take pleasure in the magnificent standing field of the variety *Seven Wonders of the World*.' It must have been a sunny day when the picture was taken, judging by the shadows beneath and between the bushes. The embankment of the local railroad forms the horizon of the picture; above it rear the tops of several fruit trees, over which light clouds hang. So there they stand in the magnificently standing field of potatoes, the woman's arm in the man's, content, and the potatoes bloom. The air must certainly have been shimmering above the embankment of the local railroad. It's on just such Turneresque days that occasional roses are still blooming in the gardens of Amrain, long-stemmed, so to speak decadent, as you can come across them in Indian summer at the foot of the south façades of the hotel-palaces on the quay in Lucerne," Baur said.

He blew his nose. A newspaper lifted up from the asphalt, fluttered after a car, settled down again. A pair of crows flew toward the woods that here grew close to the other side of the Gösger-strasse; they turned off, flew around the spherical tank, landed on the spherical tank, cawed on the spherical tank, at least one of them cawed, while the other tripped mincingly back and forth, nervously raising one or the other wing; whereupon the pair took off, to disappear for good into the woods.

"I no longer have that sketch of the Burghölzli, but I'll go there sometime anyway, to wander around where my father lived with the insane for more than thirty years. He worked in the Observation Hall, so he must have observed the incoming patients for a while in order to write reports on his observations. And then I'd like to try to recall his vacations, especially those from the time when Benno was running a small farm at home. I'd like to see my father before me, striding through a field of grain with the scythe on his shoulder to mow a stand of wheat in the field beyond; or the way he stood before the mirror in the room downstairs to shave, to comb his hair (nervously), while I was happy he was going away, leaving me to my contemplation again, to the plums, hens, trees, in winter skating, going sleigh riding, or curling.

"We got the stones for curling from the processor of pig intestines, who even imported pig instestines from India. This presumably meant that we also came into possession of Indian curling stones. We made the handles for them from old bicycle tires, but the nails occasionally made them split open on the side, which could lead to our having to get new stones. But the stones were, so to speak, in short supply. To get the stones going called for steep inclines, so that for us it depended above all on the fertile depressions on the slopes, those hollows that reveal that ages ago grapes too grew in Amrain.

"Apropos the mirror: before the same one (I don't know where it got to when the property was divided) Johanna also stood as she got ready to act as *Helvetia* in the hospital bazaar (on a horse-drawn float covered with flowers). She stood motionless on the flowery float as it moved through the town. Even people from the surrounding villages had come. And years later people were still talking about this *Helvetia*. Above all she impressed the men, the young ones. Six paces northeast of the mirror, which on occasion also reflected the Christmas tree standing diagonally opposite on the large table, I noticed the smell of my confirmation shoes, whose color I encounter again every autumn in chestnuts freed from their shells. This brown immediately brings to mind again the smell of my confirmation shoes and that image six paces northeast of the mirror, the image of a youth in a blue confirmation suit—holding brown shoes in his hands," Baur said.

I thought of how on the Gösgerstrasse Baur held the chestnut leaf by its stem, turning it this way and that, simulating a fluttering hen, a *Man with Hen*.

"Postcards were stuck in the mirror's frame along with the few letters that came. Later these things sometimes got behind the mirror, since it was placed against the corner between two walls, forming an acute angle that received mail, at least the discarded mail, which gave the mirror an added significance, for this mail occasionally contained something important," said Baur, following the car of the potential truck purchasers as it disappeared up ahead heading for Gösgen.

One couldn't avoid thinking about the potential truck purchasers, which led one to envision certain internal organs in cross section, through which wine and cutlets were pleased to take their customary course. One arrived again at Baur and what he had said, that people's excretions or odors presumably meant the same thing to flowers that the odors of flowers meant to people.

"Bindschädler, it can happen that these days, when I sit down of an evening on the west side of the garden shed, the sky looks violet down below, turning wine-red and then pink toward the zenith. Against this background the tops of the cherry trees are watercolor filigree. These aren't any old cherry trees, but the ones under which Anna had taken refuge when they seized her to shove her into a psychiatric clinic. A policeman, a chauffeur, a doctor, and the council secretary were the captors.

"Later Anna came back, on foot and in a nightgown. Not for long, of course.

"Earlier, behind Anna's house, we used to sled on the hillside. One evening a neighbor's kid, standing on the sled, carved a track in the snow. In the morning he put the sled in the frozen track and rode off without steering.

"Later, at the railroad station in Amrain, with the help of a string, he set the flap of his cap in motion, as a soldier among soldiers.

"Months later he came back—at night, on foot, without shoes and without staying."

I walked somewhat more slowly. Baur kept pace. Every day the heart pumps twelve thousand liters of blood, I thought, three hundred twenty million during a lifetime. That would fill eight thousand tank trucks. The heart pumps a whole life long without being serviced. It pumps on average two and a half billion times. A car motor with servicing manages a hundred and fifty million piston strokes. Then it's ready for the scrap heap.

Baur blew his nose, slowly passing the handkerchief back and forth under his nose while he looked at the woods, which, as mentioned, in this place come close to the north side of the Gösgerstrasse.

"In Amrain, Bindschädler, there was in Albert Baur's time (who almost always had the stump of a cigar sticking in his face and lightly rolled his tongue in speaking, which made his sentences sound rounded off, at least as far as modulation was concerned), in Amrain there was in Albert Baur's time (and not even very far from his establishment) the master butcher, farmer, and cattle dealer Joachim Schwarz. He also managed the egg dealer's large field south of our property. In the apple orchard in this field there were forget-me-nots with large flowers. Presumably that had something to do with the chicken manure. It was important for Joachim Schwarz to manure his fields, and he had plenty of manure, for he added the leftovers from slaughtering (blood, entrails) to his manure preparation, that is to say he enriched the manure derived from his agricultural endeavors with the leftovers mentioned, which increased the content of the derived manure, upon which the enriched content could be diluted by adding water. Joachim Schwarz had four or five manure wagons. Their tanks were placed low, hung between the back wheels, so to speak. Up front was a box for the wagon driver. Then they, his drivers, formed manure processions, drove with four, five manure wagons onto the egg dealer's large field. And the grasses and flowers must certainly have rejoiced whenever these processions approached.

But with time only buttercups were left. And the field, at least when the grass was going to seed, presented a yellow surface.

"Bindschädler, so it came about that Joachim Schwarz orchestrated the procession of his four, five manure wagons, that is, with his drivers, horses, while in Baur's attic the clocks ticked, brother-in-law Ferdinand cooked fir trees, Father strode through wheat fields, the cherry tree (about which brother-in-law Ferdinand said: 'I no longer let my cherry trees get so tall. I saw them all off on top. I don't want any more tall cherry trees') was bringing its cherries to ripeness—that during all that Philipp was painting a façade, that of the country house at Langenthal (which I just recently glimpsed again from the local train, if only for moments).

"At that time the wind still blew through two elms in the cemetery. And here was where my father was moldering. In the meantime he has been cleared off, that is, the gravestone has been leveled. The grave of Lina, Philipp's first wife, is also gone.

"Philipp had been trained in a painting and decorating shop in Amrain. I went to school with one of the sons of this business's owner. He had a talent for painting. Even today, on my march through Amrain, looking at the curve of a roof pediment or a poster here or there that he painted, I have to think of Georg, who lives in Australia now but who was in Amrain on a visit a little while ago," Baur said.

Meanwhile we were walking faster again. I held back a little. Baur slackened his pace without letting on. The sun was shining. I unbuttoned two, three buttons of my coat. The ground rose gently. The heart owes its endurance to its good lubrication by secretions, I thought. These are produced by the heart sac. The heart muscle is the pumping engine. As the heart muscle stretches and compresses the empty spaces it encloses, blood is driven through the circulation's system of pipes. The heart has four valves. The two that regulate the flow of blood between the upper two chambers and the lower two that only open when the filled upper chambers contract, forcing the blood into the lower chambers connected to them. The third valve opens the way for the blood to flow into the large aorta, the fourth valve opens the artery to the lungs.

"Or it could happen, Bindschädler, that one ran into Joachim Schwarz as he was standing on the bridge inspecting the parade of manure wagons returning home, four or five in number, while a swarm of doves took off, flying a horizontal figure eight over the farms, the house of the clockmaker Albert Baur as well. The mirror sheltered the image of Johanna, representing *Helvetia*, suspiciously and profoundly, while several postcards were stuck in the frame and the discarded mail was resting behind the mirror," said Baur, my former fellow soldier, to whom, as mentioned, I presented the selected works of Adalbert Stifter at Christmas during our active service, inspired really by the snow-hung firs of the Justis Valley, which always (these snow-hung firs) remind me of Adalbert Stifter, why I cannot say.

"Bindschädler, one of the drivers of those manure wagons is still alive today. In those days I occasionally saw him walking down the road on which the large field lies. Once I came upon him standing at the top of this field to which they had driven manure, four, five wagons at the same time, a column of manure vehicles. He was probably thinking back to the time when one drove out with four, five special manure wagons, with a box in front, a wagon driver on it, pulled by two horses, in order to manure the egg dealer's large field with manure enriched with blood and entrails, on the other hand thinned with water. It happens that this surviving driver was the one who took blood and entrails from the slaughterhouse to the manure pits of the agricultural enterprise. But the consequence of this constant manuring was that the buttercups gained the upper hand, and at a certain point the egg dealer's large field chose to transform itself into a field of flowers that was almost Far-Eastern," Baur said, swinging his arms.

During active service he walked more erect. Has he read Stifter? I asked myself.

"On one of the cherry trees that still today are standing in the large field and along the road, one of my cousins once pulled down a branch to break off a swelling bud, and brought it to his mouth to chew. That was the coming of spring. This cousin, by the way, was the last tramp in our region. I believe he knew the Jura like no other. When he died, laid out in front of the hospital, the mountains of the Jura glowed in Indian summer splendor, and a peacock butterfly fluttered above the mourners. He had wanted to become a teacher, this cousin. It didn't work out. After his military training he went on the road, and died as a tramp on the road, at an advanced age and opposite the shed where the steam-threshing machine was stored. Bindschädler, there are hardly any peacock butterflies left. There are more skulls," Baur said.

Which made one think of the child's skull in little Meret's hands, and of the white rose.

"By one of the cherry trees out in the field my wife, who was picking cherries, suffered a sunstroke. And this cherry tree, on seeing which, as I have mentioned, Ferdinand said he no longer wanted such tall cherry trees, I have before my eyes every day, at least for moments. Today it's merely the sorry shadow of a cherry tree, occasionally visited by a woodpecker. After stormy nights, Bindschädler, stormy nights in November, after those really most terrible stormy nights of the year—during which you are afraid the tiles will start falling from the roof, for when you have an old house of your own, stormy nights are quite different, but one also realizes that they're quite steadfast, all these houses, sturdily resisting the storm—after such stormy nights in November I sit down in my garden shed, among other things to look at the cherry tree, the hacked-off, handicapped cherry tree, and then it seems as if it were concentrating on raising itself to dance on its toes, a child's toe dance. And the lichens on it glow white. And one makes an effort to realize that it's November, that the whole business with winter is yet to come, that all the tiles, which have absorbed the summer sun, even the Indian summer sun, will soon be receiving snow and ice," Baur said, reaching for his cap.

Baur looked at me. When the heart valves seize up, I said to myself, the suddenly stopped bloodstream suffers a reversal, the waves of which spread out to the wall of the heart and from there to the wall of the chest.

"On such stormy nights one imagines how the sea must rage, Bindschädler, and how the people at sea, the seafarers, must live in terror through the hours of storm. We experienced the sea that way twice, on Kos. It was a glorious day. Only the wind was blowing, an old seafarer's wind. We had to entrust ourselves to a boat that always, when we were wandering about the harbor, gave one an unpleasant feeling. A Greek, seventy, seventy-five, dark-skinned, with a death's-head face, was its captain. A port official came on board, counted the passengers. That was not the usual practice on other boats. We set out to sea. Hardly had we left the harbor when it began. The Greek looked to me like the ferryman to Hell. He handled the helm coolly. Occasionally his actions were rash. The passengers were mute. Children threw up in paper bags. Grown-ups tried to get to the railing to vomit into the sea. One dug one's fingers into one's seat. One braced oneself against the towering waves. One tried to assist the boat by shifting one's weight, which was of course stressful, this constant balancing, this incessant if strained attempt to help determine the boat's reactions. One looked around, rolling one's eyes. One asked oneself whether one would make it. One said to oneself that swimmers survive seven minutes, non-swimmers four. One was upset about the borrowed camera. One tuned out.—Bindschädler, a Dutch couple was sitting behind us, they laughed when a huge swell came, their laughter increased up to the moment when the boat threatened to capsize, diminished as it righted itself—and so on. I would gladly have turned around to box these peoples' ears. But I had to help with the boat's motions through my balancing acts, had to at least stand by the boat morally when its side rose up, which demanded my concentration. And when the boat came through, making it up the slope of the wave, then the task was to overcome its new tipping by again shifting one's weight, to catch it, as it were, to avoid capsizing. Finally we approached the island, came into its lee. One entered the peaceful harbor," Baur said. He took off his cap, passed his right hand slowly over his skull, with an expression as if listening.

The heart muscle needs blood, I told myself. A special system of arteries supplies the heart muscle. These vessels enclose the heart like a wreath.

"Bindschädler, it's a devilish business when death plays cat and mouse with one. But who doesn't know that?

"I think, when it has struck, then it's different. One has heard of people who were already gone but were somehow brought back—one has heard from these people that death is felt as highly desirable. And that a lot of light is part of it.

"In our case, on the other hand, the first gulps of water would have to be sucked into the lungs. Only then would the camera (the borrowed one) be forgotten," Baur said, coughing. He reached for his handkerchief, held it up to his nose, sneezed.

I buttoned up my coat.

"It's probably the case that ultimately God is not love, but light," Baur said, his glances spreading over the contours of the Jura, which from our vantage point appeared rather turbulent.

"Love produces new life, Bindschädler. Love is a fire with lot of light all around it . . . A lot of light is part of death too," Baur said.

I thought of the crickets. At the time, behavioral researchers were interested in their songs. They wanted to find out what *notes* they sang in order to gain some insight into the workings of their tiny nervous systems. The first results of this *philharmonic muscle orchestra* were now available.

I used to think that the chirping in my ears came from the hustle and bustle of the universe. Today I think that this chirping is distant songs, siren songs of crickets from the Beyond.

"That business about death and light has been authenticated, Bindschädler," Baur said.

An opening in the clouds appeared above the Jura, revealing a depth filled with light such as you find in the paintings of Caspar David Friedrich.

"Light plays an immense role, one might say. Also the light that springs from the fires of the loins, as it were. For where would people be without these fires?" Baur said, smiling, as I perceived out of the corner of my left eye, for my attention was directed at a gull that was just then passing the open space in the clouds, becoming smaller and black.

"In November there are often moments, especially after stormy nights, when a light appears that reminds one of the other light.

"And also, Bindschädler, when you consider what significance profane light has in painting, of landscape, our closest environment. I remember a tea room above a plaza of plane trees: March 21, the sun setting, its rays from time to time in playful rivalry with the light from the sconces, which were made of brass and accordion-pleated fabric, while distant funfair music mingled with it, which had the effect that the light, the twilight, for its part, was also trying to enter into playful rivalry with the music, which so to speak appeared to be coming from Russian funfairs, or at least from far away, while the twilight made the colors of the wood, the carpets, china, women's dresses, women's hair, fingernail polish, the varnish of the paneling, sound loud or soft, depending on the position of the passing clouds," Baur said.

Meanwhile the gull had settled on the Aare. In place of the opening there was now cloud cover.

"If the light comes from the fires in the loins or from the November sun, casting its cone of light on a group of birch trees whose trunks, branches phosphorize, even on the aforementioned cherry tree that is standing there with furrowed bark, after a stormy night, in the attitude of a child with upraised arms starting a toe dance; or whether it comes from locomotives, bicycles, Harley-Davidsons: it's always the light of another light, Bindschädler," Baur said, shoving his cap around. A train was crossing the Iron Bridge, which set off an iron spectacle. One's eyes followed it until it disappeared. The spectacle was extinguished in the tunnel.

"So all of our dead would have the light, while here on earth their bones molder away, beautifully arranged (insofar as they were not given over to the flames), letting November pass over them, and the army of the stars, until they have become dust. Dust from other dust, to blossom in a daisy, a lily, or simply in grass, to be eaten by a cow and to be excreted again or get into milk, then to be drunk by a beautiful woman nursing a beautiful infant at her breast, who soon enjoys the grass, daisies, lilies, but later suffers from burning loins, which again produce infants, who as grown-ups attempt to defy storms, even those of the sea, of November nights.—

"Bindschädler, God is light," Baur said.

Scabs were drifting across the sky. And when they broke off, a pink surface showed underneath.

Baur stuck his left hand in his pants pocket, his right into the pocket of his jacket, staring at the asphalt as if he were interested in its cracks, gray tones.

I thought of steam locomotives, North American, early models. At the same time considered the construction of the Iron Bridge. Then looked at the second railway bridge, of different construction. Then we turned into the promenade along the Aare that leads to Olten. Beeches hem the promenade, at least as far as the Trimbach Bridge and the nearby street, while directly along the water oaks, maples, acacias stand, occasionally too a chestnut, hornbeam. And one really had to force oneself to dismiss hallucinatory images of Indians in canoes. Gulls, wild ducks, loons, swans, and boats enlivened the surface of the water.

One stopped, placed both hands on the top of the railing, stared into the water, paying attention to the mirrorings, the reflections of light.

A pair of wild ducks lifted off the water, clapping their wings, flew up the Aare more or less at the height of the oaks, came down just before the Trimbach Bridge, let themselves drift.

"Bindschädler, so Johanna was representing *Helvetia* back then, at the hospital bazaar, a radiant *Helvetia*, surrounded by flowers. It was a great day.—And now this Johanna came here, together with Julia and Gisela, each with a bundle of winter asters on her arm, wearing dark clothes, in order to give news of graves. And then some of those whose graves they had visited were there again in our midst, around the table. And we exchanged gestures, glances, now and then a smile. Brother-in-law Ferdinand said that he had really succeeded in keeping his cherry trees low. One tried, in this case, to suppress a smile. And father told of his marches through Bukovina. And Lina reminded us that she had loved Philipp exactly as he had been and that it had hurt her deeply to leave him, but the headaches had gotten too bad.—Then cherry blossoms sailed over the funeral procession just before the bend in the road.

"Bindschädler, one wasn't quite sure whether Julia recognized that she was in the parental house. And you know, down in the street she asked about the name of a tree that fleecy clouds happened to be hanging over.

"One accompanied the three women with winter asters to the bend in the road.

"It was afterward that one found *Three Women with Winter Asters* as a painting on the east wall of the soul, in large format and opposite the *Field full of Bones* depicting the components of old switches, signal-boxes, axles, bumping blocks," Baur said.

Gaining height with hurried flapping of their wings, a pair of swans flew away, down the Aare. At the bend in the river they disappeared from our sight.

We let go of the top of the railing and we strolled off, beside each other, occasionally stumbling over bumps caused by tree roots under the asphalt.

Baur swung his arms, snapping his thumb and ring finger now and then, sometimes staring at the tops of the oaks, sometimes at the river. Then it seemed as if his field of view encompassed the host of the children of light.

A locomotive whistled. Train cars coupled. Which made me think of the souvenir locomotive standing in front of the workshop of the Swiss National Railways. Its silver wheel rims came to mind, its copper pipes, lanterns, numbers, above all the number of the tender. I recalled the trains across the prairie, the trains on the trans-Siberian stretch, but also the trains of manure that were said to have moved through Amrain toward the great field of the egg dealer, brought onto the scene by Joachim Schwarz, who was supposed to have once stood on the bridge, his butcher's apron flecked with blood tied around him, one corner pinned up, while in the clockmaker's attic room the clocks must have been ticking, racing one another, each having the insane impulse to be the first to tick away time in Amrain.

Baur leaned toward a chestnut tree at the edge of the promenade. He stopped, observed it for a while, said: "Look at that brown! Of course it's most beautiful when the chestnut comes fresh from the shell. But it's still a glorious brown, and varied, too. Every autumn I take two, three chestnuts and distribute them in the left pockets of my better jackets. That way I am reminded throughout the whole year of the time of chestnuts, of the time of chrysanthemums, Bindschädler, that's what a dreamer I am!"

One laughed, noted the masses of water parading by, observed the oak tree beside one, its bizarre top.

We left the promenade, climbed the steps leading to the Trimbach Bridge, crossed the bridge, which was supported by a not exactly graceful concrete arch slightly raised in the center, the railings wrought-iron bars in the form of wrought-iron circles that were divided in star fashion by wrought-iron bars. At the end of the bridge we turned left into the Quaistrasse, walking along the bank of the Aare under old trees interspersed with hollies and other shrubs; strolled, crossing the Quaistrasse, into the Fahrweg, which runs parallel to the south façade of the old hospital, where in the back gardens of the residential blocks south of the street an almost unbroken row of hydrangeas stands, blooming in various colors.

"For me this is on one hand the street of hydrangeas, while on the other I think of the old hospital as if it were Tolstoy's house in Yasnaja Polyana, which the children's-book lindens (thick trunks with peacock fans) along the street emphasize. Tolstoy is said to have inherited the enormous estate from his mother, Princess Volkonsky," Baur said, staring at the façade that shimmered brightly through the shrubs of the garden.

I repeated "Yasnaja Polyana" to myself and found that its sound was really marvelous. But then I thought of the little house on the Ulica Dabrowiecka in Warsaw, and thought that the Varsovians should have had the luck to save in daring fashion all the documents needed to reconstruct their city: copper engravings, drawings, paintings, not least the perspectives of the Italian Belotto, who called himself Canaletto and who lived in Warsaw at the end of the eighteenth century. But above all, the exact measurements. In the years from 1923 to 1939 it was customary for architecture students in Warsaw to survey and draw historical buildings for practice. This material was first walled up in the basement of an institute, and then with the help of collaborating Germans taken to a monastery. So after the war one had the plans for almost all the buildings at a scale of 1:50.

After that I abandoned myself to the feeling of being freed from all the things of this earth. Sucked in the air, as dogs do when it is spring and evening and the wild beckons, so to speak.

"Bindschädler, I've thought a whole life long of writing.—Without wanting to torture you now with my views on literature, I still must say that for me a novel can be compared to a carpet, a hand-woven carpet, in creating which special attention is paid to the colors and motifs, which repeat themselves, varied of course, handmade, marked almost by a certain ponderousness, and which reminds one of a girl from school days and a field of flowers with cherry trees in it that are just blossoming; one would like to be walking across this field of flowers at least once more, and of course not alone," Baur said.

Meanwhile we were approaching the Baslerstrasse, which was filled with traffic. Facing us was the Hagberg, at its foot a garage. The Hagberg is a hill that rises some thirty meters above the surrounding terrain and is wooded. A children's playground is on its western side. The Baslerstrasse goes over the Jura to Basel.

"When in November the early light chases the green of the slopes into one's cheeks, Bindschädler, it can happen that the aforementioned cherry tree looks as if it had lain long in the sea, for then its bark resembles the surface of Greek vases that have lain for millennia in the Aegean, which is where Kos also lies, Kos with its homes and businesses, vivid Hawaiian flowers, salt-meadows and Persian lilacs, but above all with its old women, who sit clad in black before the entrances to their houses in the shade of Persian lilacs, talking with the dead.

"In my thoughts I occasionally wander across the Freedom Square in Kos, Bindschädler, see the market arcade, whose central space contains the vegetable and fruit stands, and around it the shops of the butchers, fishmongers, dealers in spirits, and other merchants. There's even a toilet. Its stench can be detected from afar. Old Greeks rise up before me, Greeks in pantaloons and boots, picking their noses under shade trees behind the market, drinking Greek coffee, reminiscing about old times, great times of course," Baur said.

We crossed the Baslerstrasse on the zebra stripes opposite the city park; went back a stretch and turned left into the Hagbergstrasse, which at first runs along the northeast side of the city park, gently rising. We took the Promenade, which in the city park runs parallel to the Hagbergstrasse. Suddenly we were standing before the bronze bust of Nicolaus Riggenbach, who lived from 1817 to 1899, and among other things busied himself with constructing locomotives.

Baur and I stopped in front of the bust, which towered above a square pedestal of black marble that tapered as it rose, the pedestal itself resting on a granite plinth surrounded by pansies.

Nicolaus Riggenbach must have had a forceful face, a real countenance, a face whose bronze features led one to infer energy, creativity, endurance, wit, and intelligence, qualities that must have absolutely provoked him to build locomotives. The city park or garden presented itself as parks usually do: natural-artificial, tinged with a certain melancholy, even sadness, but which in this case could be ignored. The pieces on the chessboard beneath the trees were left to themselves, not far from a bed of roses that still showed isolated blossoms.

We arrived at the Schöngrundstrasse. On its northwest side are two art nouveau houses, about which we began to talk.

I said to Baur that in the summer of 1935 Count Harry Kessler noted in his diary, on the Rambla de San José in Barcelona (with its celebrated flower stalls): trees, flowers, all plants were the only earthly things that are blessed, whose natural state is what we call heavenly bliss. Plants were altogether far more perfect beings, seen from the divine perspective, than people. They experienced no Fall of Man, are and remain without sin, apparently without pain as well. (Today one believes we have discovered that plants do experience pain, even anxiety.) There is a profound truth in paradise being represented as a garden, as a place whose life is plant life, and where man as such is and remains a stranger. The Fall of Man, the expulsion of man from paradise, signifies his irretrievable separation from the perfect, divine, vegetative life.—This diary entry is a late echo, but once again the authentic voice, of the generation of around 1900. How in plant life sharp individuation has been done away with, unique forms appearing only in transition, the clear line dissolved in favor of the welling up, the wildly proliferating, the intertwining; thus the external appearance of art nouveau exhibits no unambiguous features. Art nouveau was the expression of a conscious turning away from the decadent feeling of the fin de siècle, a turning away from the signs of decay in society and art; proclaiming the comprehensive renewal of life, but on the other hand remaining prisoner of the heritage it was trying to overcome, and sharing important features with it. One of the leading ideas of art nouveau was the proliferation of ornament. The home was to be the place where beauty was a cult, sign of the rediscovered unity of body and spirit, life and art.

Baur, his left hand in his pants pocket, his right in his jacket pocket, was walking leaning slightly forward, as if he were again finding the cracks in the asphalt especially interesting.

We turned left into the Bannstrasse, which runs perpendicular to the Schöngrundstrasse, then left again into the Feigelstrasse and right into the Grundstrasse; walked along the Blumenweg to the Bleichmattstrasse, which brought us in a southeasterly direction to the Martinskirche, St. Martin's Church, which involved crossing the Ziegelfeldstrasse, busy with traffic. We entered the twin-towered Martinskirche, a building from the turn of the century, passing grimacing stone faces at the entrance. In the church, the Bible lay open. While Baur walked around looking at the paintings, the stained glass, I read in the chapter at the opened page, Ezekiel 37: "The hand of the Lord was upon me, and carried me out in the Spirit of the Lord, and set me down in the midst of the valley which was full of bones. And He caused me to pass by them round about: and behold, there were very many in the open valley; and lo, they were very dry. And he said unto me, Son of man, can these bones live? And I answered, O Lord God, thou knowest.

"Again he said unto me, Prophesy upon these bones, and say unto them, O ye dry bones, hear the word of the Lord. Thus saith the Lord God unto these bones: Behold, I will cause breath to enter into you, and ye shall live: And I will lay sinews upon you, and will bring up flesh upon you, and cover you with skin, and put breath in you, and ye shall live; and ye shall know that I am the Lord.

"So I prophesied as I was commanded: and as I prophesied, there was a noise, and behold a shaking, and the bones came together, bone to its bone. And when I beheld, lo, the sinews and the flesh came up upon them, and the skin covered them above: but there was no breath in them. Then He said unto me, Prophesy unto the wind, prophesy, son of man, and say to the wind, Thus saith the Lord God; Come from the four winds, O breath, and breathe upon the slain, that they may live. So I prophesied as He commanded me, and the breath came into them, and they lived, and stood up upon their feet, an exceeding great army."

Baur was looking at the enormous stained-glass rose window.

The fence of palings came to my mind, the curved row of maple trees, the ones with the ball-shaped tops that in spring bring forth yellow-red flower structures like art nouveau, and that in the fall abandon their leaves to the wind, one by one, sometimes in a swarm, holding back this or that single leaf at the top of the crown, on which they flap like the small flags at late festivals.

Baur, his hands still in his pockets, was at that moment walking down the aisle. The tops of the row ends left and right formed imposing ornaments, which became perspectively narrower toward the exit, while the ornaments were repeatedly mirrored in the waxed tiles, almost like pictures painted on the back of glass. Winter asters were standing in front of the altar, pastel-colored, in great bouquets. Behind them yellow, large-blossomed chrysanthemums had been placed.

I followed Baur, told him that I had just read about the *Field full of Bones*.

In the baptistery, that is, to the left of the baptistery (at least as one leaves) there is a niche, like a chapel, where the sitting Mary is holding in her arms Jesus brought down from the cross, lying across her lap so that the spear wound in the right side of his chest is visible. All day long a twilight lies over the whole, which particularly emphasizes the sculpture's pastel coloring.

We approached this sculpture, at some distance of course. I noticed that Baur was apparently trying to get a view of Jesus's spear wound through the ring of decorative railing around the stoup. I remembered Baur's saying that he had thought a whole life long of writing. And he appeared before me as he had after he said that, when on the spot he had slowly raised the heel of his right foot, set it down, raised it, and so forth, with an expression as if listening.

We left the Martinskirche, but not before I thought of an orchestra rehearsal that I had attended once by chance at which baroque Christmas music was performed, walked, after the Konradstrasse, through the Ringstrasse, crossed the Munzingerplatz, which features a grove of chestnut trees and at times serves as a market, at other times as a parking lot, passing the Stadtkirche too, in order to see the three paintings by Gubler in the museum on the Kirchgasse: paintings produced at the edge of madness and, as it were, at the final moment.

As we climbed the steps of the museum I told Baur that a painter friend of mine, Fritz Strebel, said that he had once run into Gubler in the art museum in Basel, and since they knew one another, Gubler and Strebel, he would have liked to have greeted Gubler quite cordially. But Gubler had hidden behind his wife the way children are accustomed to hiding themselves behind their mothers' skirts.

Arrived at the top floor, we were standing directly in front of the three Gubler paintings: on the left a still-life of relatively small format, in the middle a landscape with the Schlieren gasworks, on the right a self-portrait, done in tones of red. I pointed out that from a particular spot one could see these three paintings separately in one's field of vision. One placed oneself there. Stood there for a time.

We only looked quickly at the other paintings on this floor, descended the stairs, were carried away by the rooms of the parterre, where we happened upon an exhibit of Solothurn landscapes from the nineteenth century; left the museum, walked past the Stadtkirche, and followed the Baslerstrasse, then the Froburgstrasse, to arrive at the EPA department store.

It occurred to me that Baur was a careless pedestrian. More than once I had to hold him back to keep him from being run over by a car.

In the restaurant of the EPA, which had something bare, almost antiseptic about it, but in inexplicable fashion reminded one of the turn of the century, we sat down at one of the round tables after getting some coffee and pastry. One remained lost in one's thoughts for a considerable time.

"Bindschädler, after we had that ominous boat trip behind us, the inhabitants of the island seemed like children of light. First we had a small refreshment, it was just mealtime, then went into the village, and on the way to the Greek Orthodox chapel we were called over by a young woman to come sit with her on her veranda. She cut a large bunch of grapes from over the veranda, washed it in a bowl, laid it on a plate, and placed it in front of us. Greek folk music on the radio came from inside through the open window.

"The Aegean wind brushed the grape leaves. With a guilty conscience one pushed a coin under the bowl. We left. In the Greek Orthodox chapel the cleric explained the icons. One took photographs, went to the cemetery. The borders of the few graves were whitewashed. The objects on the graves were also whitewashed. The crosses were made out of boards. Here and there on the graves were something like dog houses, tinted blue, also bluish white. A few avicennia provided shade. A few palms as well. One took more photographs, then left the grounds of the chapel to go to a hilltop chapel, from which there was an unhindered view of the sea and the interior of the island. In the distance you could make out, at the foot of a hill, a wood of stone pine, which in the ochre of the terrain appeared (one might almost say) legendary.

"In the alleys again, one realized that here too everything was whitewashed except for some window frames, some steps, which were blue.

"In the beach café one drank the local wine, then went to the boat and went aboard, with a gloomy premonition.—And truly: after about half an hour's journey the boat suddenly shifted on its side so that one feared capsizing.

"Arrived on Kos, one enjoyed the sight of the fortress, the huge rubber tree, the palms, yachts, women, the young tourist girls, and had above all a still sharper eye for the women at the entrance to their houses who speak with their dead for hours, at midday, in the shade of the pines, palms, of the Persian lilacs," Baur said.

Clouds passed above the roofs, occasionally allowing a glimpse of pink-colored expanses. They drifted eastward, as it were like the scab of an enormous wound.

I went to the coatrack, put on my coat. Baur clapped on his cap, after having likewise wiped his mouth with his napkin. We went downstairs, on the second floor made our way through the artificial flowers, for now there were many people around, curious onlookers for the most part; paid attention to the iris, reflexively smelled the lilacs, ran our fingers through the forsythia blossoms, counted the colors of the tulips, recoiled from the sunflowers standing palely yellow in a pot on the floor. Additional light poured from the corner with lamps, the lamp department.

One positioned oneself on the escalator, walked past the counter with ear, neck, and finger accessories, watches too. Passed the counter with soap, toothpaste, hand and hair creams, perfume whose scents were imitations of hyacinths, for example, myrrh, lavender, the scents of lilies, violets, thyme, even of jasmine (which always reminds one of District Administrator Trotta, who at the time of the jasmine's flowering, which is also that of chestnuts, strode through the allées of Schönbrunn to ask Kaiser Franz Josef pardon for his son), perfumes whose scents were designed to mask the odors of the body; looked at the salesgirl behind the cosmetics counter, and passed the counter of music cassettes, reaching the open air through an acoustic drizzle.

On the walk beside the Aare we were accompanied by two figures, who were in shop windows, only one of which swung its arms.

Under the impression that in the Olten EPA everything was smooth, white, tall, and quite manageable, almost sterile, an impression probably reinforced by the plastic lamps in the upstairs restaurant, and on the second floor the stand with the artificial irises, chrysanthemums, blossoming chestnut branches, we walked in the direction of the Aare or the train station, on whose rear there is a clock, up above in a gable, showing a quarter to three and reminding one of Albert Baur's clocks, ticking for all they were worth, striving to overtake one another in order to be the first to tick Amrain's time.

Shortly before the Bahnhofbrücke we crossed the Froburgstrasse on the zebra stripes, which took some patience, then crossed the Amthausquai as well, in order to walk upstream on the river promenade, but then Baur sat down on one of the benches, his hands in his pockets. I went over to the platform with the weather column, observed Zielemp Castle, looked downriver, where the view was much more open, cast a glance at Baur, who was staring straight ahead, suddenly saw that oil painting in which a child is depicted in a pale green damask dress whose hem is spread out in a large circle and conceals the feet, around the body a gold chain with a loop that reaches down to the floor in front, on her head a crownlike ornament of gold and silver sequins, woven through with silk threads and pearls, holding the skull of a child and a white rose.

In the meantime Baur had pulled his right hand from his jacket pocket and placed it on the arm of the bench. He looked over at me, smiling, indicating the sky with upward glances: "Glorious!—Whether the November sun is aiming beams of light, phosphorescent ones, at a group of pear trees, as mentioned, or at a hillside that turns it *green* here and there, or whether they strike the Aare, its banks, promenades, trees, the train station, a Renaissance façade, the light always wants to make you believe that November is really *everything*, so to speak the peak of the year, it outdoes spring, summer, blazing winter—everything. Yes!"

Baur watched a pair of wild ducks just flying over the Bahnhofbrücke in a long-drawn-out arc. I recalled the blowfly that got caught in the web, struggled free (after it had previously reached a stand-off with its captor, upon which the spider—casting one or two loops around one of the blowfly's legs—withdrew), only to fall immediately thereafter onto the web of a fully grown spider, which got into a violent duel with the blowfly, coming at it from below and behind and biting it: while beams of light were falling now on this, now on that part of the staffage, and also on a group of pear trees as well. The siren of an ambulance reverberated from the other bank. Later it turned onto the Bahnhofbrücke, disappeared down the Froburgstrasse in the direction of the hospital.

Baur, his left hand in his pants pocket, his left leg slung over the right, his right arm lying on the back of the bench, looked into the light.

I grasped the wrought-iron railing of the platform, observed the waves, their play of reflections, looked at a magnolia tree, remembered its flowers, said to myself that those too really had something smooth, rigid, almost sterile about them, turned around, read: "The donor of this weather column, Nicolaus Riggenbach: Born May 2, 1817, in Gebweiler. Schools in Basel. Technical apprentice in Lyon and Paris. From 1840 active in the Kessler engineering works in Karlsruhe, above all in the construction of locomotives. 1853 appointed by the central management of the railways as head of the workshops in Olten. 1871 Vitznau-Rigi railroad. Honorary citizen of Olten, Trimbach, Aarau. Died in Olten on July 24, 1899."

Now a compact field of clouds pushed forward. A gull circled over the promenade, screamed once, screamed a second time, landed nearby on the wrought-iron railing, facing upstream, eyed its surroundings, took off, landed on the Aare, let itself drift under the Bahnhofbrücke, striving to keep its glance directed upstream.

Looking over at Baur, I realized that he was looking downstream and apparently observing the statue at the head of the bridge, representing a bronze horse with a rider, that is, a bronze man who was just on the point of mounting the horse.

And one thought to oneself that the horse really—unlike most other animals—belongs to man and that there must be a lot of them in Heaven, according to the Book of Revelation, which speaks somewhere of an army on white horses.

And one thought to oneself further that the horse has shared the fate of people, especially their so-called great destiny, which had usually been accompanied by the sounds of horns and trumpets. And one thought how horses can now and then assume a position of staring into the distance as if they were dreaming, remembering; whereupon they beat a circle in the air with their tails, push up their rumps, run away, reach down for a clump of grass, lift their heads, in order to dreamingly remember again.

As sculptures they frequently look rather awkward, rather big too, these horses of bronze.

It had become cooler.

Baur stood up, leaving his left hand in his pants pocket, put his right hand in his jacket pocket, brought his upper body slightly forward, his head as well, asked "Shall we go?" simultaneously setting himself in motion, upstream.

On the promenade, shaded by lindens, we approached the former Zielemp Castle; pointed out to each other details of a façade covered with images that now appeared. Now and then a linden leaf sailed down, one of which came to rest at the feet of a woman clothed in black who was sitting on one of the benches on the promenade. I said that as for the building on the left, it happened to be the former Zielemp Castle, which had been turned into various stores, at least on the ground floor, a boutique for example, a delicatessen, farther on a theater as well, an optician's, a gun shop, and so forth. On the right side of the street there was also a boutique, then a camera store, then a picture framer's. In the meantime, in the Zielempgasse we actually passed by the display window with guns inside, knives, approached the Alte Brücke. At the moment the small square in front of the bridge was in sunlight, which reminded one that it was St. Martin's Day, November 11, 1977, and that to judge by the weather one could look forward to a St. Martin's summer, an Indian summer.

Baur remained tight-lipped.

Instead of now going across the Alte Brücke we strolled right, into the Hauptgasse, in order to get to the Mühlegasse at its end, with the Stadtkirche before us; at the bottom of the Mühlegasse crossed the Dünnern, which brings water from the Jura into the Aare nearby, on the Schützenmatt reached the grove of plane trees, which is especially dear to me since the time it melded into Bartók's *Concerto for Orchestra*, weaving in the sound metamorphically, almost as a ballet, the grove finding its way back to its natural state only after Bartok's orchestral work had faded away and the night beyond the windows was again an ordinary night. I told Baur about it.

We walked through the grove of plane trees, detoured around a building that apparently served as a gymnasium, raised up in brick. But its walls, a large expanse, were stuccoed. Only the entrance and window frames were visible as brickwork.

One passed one's fingers over the stucco.

"Bindschädler, one can't make out what's going on inside one, all the things that are going on within when you abandon yourself to music. So it can happen, as you said, that Bartók's *Concerto for Orchestra* can bring a grove of plane trees into oneself, where it turns into a ballet of plane trees, absorbing the sky, its light, its clouds and wind together with the sounds, forming a complicated choreographic composition of an unfamiliar kind, of unusual extent as well. Yes!

"Thus, Bindschädler, one could say that Bartók's music brings groves of plane trees to ballet dancing, bringing in what's around them, while prayer moves mountains or wakes the dead, even when their bones lie neatly ordered in the earth, which, according to the usual opinion, is the right place for them," Baur said.

We followed the path across the Dünnern meadow. Antonioni's tennis scene from *Blow-Up* came to mind, which was mimed, without a tennis ball; saw the green of the court, which in the light from the searchlights appeared especially green.

Passing the boathouse we reached the river promenade, walked upstream without talking, crossed the pedestrian walkway of the Gäubahnbrücke, which is fastened on the side to the stone piers and covered with woven wire, apparently on account of hard objects that might be thrown from trains just when a passerby is on the walkway. The fir trees of the Justis Valley came to one's mind, and, with a glance at Baur, the episode on the hillside, where Baur had brushed off Bütikofer's army tunic after Bütikofer—pulling up his pants—had slipped.

"Bindschädler, when in November the first snow falls on the roofs of my cousins, on the roofs of the properties of my former or dead cousins, that is, when one morning snow lies on the roofs of those places that sheltered my brothers and sisters, and when snow lies under the pear trees—insofar as it reaches them, for it frequently happens that this thin layer of new snow does not get to lie beneath the trees, especially if they are standing in the wind, for somehow their tops, even when they are bare, without leaves, and basically quite permeable, protect the ground under the trees so that oval green spots remain, which look as if green shadows are lying on the snow; whereas on the other hand, where a tree, let's say a pear tree, is protected from the wind, the snow extends right up to its trunk, and because the grass (bright green grass, in contrast to the snow) stands relatively upright, the snow cover comes to lie on the grass, which gives the surface a gossamer texture, like that of spread-out sheep's fleece.

"Of course this snow cover on the grass is much more fine-spun than sheep's fleece. And, as mentioned, the green of the grass is in this case especially green; and right away one sees in one's mind the first snowdrops or daffodils, which is really something like a hallucination, but that's part of it: nature, landscape, animals, plants, are always, apparently, a good three months ahead, for where would it lead if in St. Martin's Indian summer buds were not budding on the trees barely after their leaves had withered, paled, been blown away by the wind—if, therefore, on such a November morning when the snow is lying on the roof tiles of my remaining cousins who are still living and on the roofs of the former houses of my dead cousins, but also on the roofs of my still living brothers and sisters, then the land, its piles of snow, trees, woods, rocks, houses, paling fences, people, appears as it were sketched, as a pencil drawing. And it smells of graphite, like the drawing studio of an art school. And the whole has the peace of a drawing about it. Yes!—And if at the same time the radio happens to be playing Brahms's piano music, which one would at first think were Chopin mazurkas or nocturnes, and one happens to pick up a page of a newspaper with a photograph captioned *Mass grave of Soviet soldiers in Stalingrad, 1943*, the grave ringed around by a temporary fence of bed frames, and if one looks at the soldier who, with lowered head, leaning slightly forward, his right hand in his coat pocket, is stealing away, presumably in the company of all those soldiers now lying beneath the earth covered by a thin layer of snow, which looks not in the least gossamer; if one observes this soldier as he walks away from this mass grave hemmed in by iron bed frames, hospital bed frames, this mass grave of his comrades, taking them with him, perhaps as a group photo in spring, with vodka, balalaikas, girls; when one observes this soldier striding off, one has the impression that he too thinks that the dead are in the right place, one has done one's duty, now they belong to the earth, are provided for," Baur said.

We had reached the Aarburgstrasse and walked in the direction of the Alte Brücke.

I thought of crickets, and that among most crickets and grasshoppers only the males sing, by stroking the strip of small teeth on one edge of the top wing against the edge of the bottom one. Their signals are for the females of their own species, which hear these songs in the great cacophony of a summer meadow. Crickets have their ears in their front legs, I said to myself, visible on a shining silvery eardrum. These hearing organs separate out the songs of other species, working as a *filter*.

Then it seemed that one was hearing seductive songs of crickets from the Beyond.—

Arrived at the Alte Brücke, we swung off to the right into the Unterführungsstrasse, went through the railroad underpass, came to the two discount stores MIGROS/ABM, which are here united under one roof, and crossed the Unterführungstrasse in order to continue walking on the other side of the street, whereupon we suddenly found ourselves standing in front of the pet store *Arakanga*, in whose window a parrot was scratching itself behind the ears; that is, at the moment it was scratching itself behind its right ear with two toes of its fettered right foot. Of course the ear was not to be seen, but its position could be inferred. The bird kept its right eye shut, its head inclined to the right, its right wing lifted away from its body. I said I was really a little in love with the word *Arakanga*, and that the Russian steppe called Karaganda had become well-known as the landing place of Russian spaceships; and that this parrot was presumably carrying out its scratching in stereotypical fashion, for I had often come upon it just as it was scratching behind its ears, that is, behind one of its ears, with two toes of its fettered right or free left foot. The ear in question was of course not to be seen, but could be inferred from its position. The parrot had closed the corresponding eye with relish, its head inclined somewhat to the right or left, one of its wings gently lifted away from the body. That reminded one of the statue with the eagle on the Bürkliplatz in Zurich.

I again tried to free myself from the things of this world; sucked in air, as dogs like to do, on a spring evening, for example when the wild calls.

"In the last century, Bindschädler, one of our clan is said to have emigrated to England and made a considerable fortune as a manufacturer without leaving any descendants. My cousin Berger, as mentioned, had time all his life to occupy himself with freeing this inheritance; so he was really only an iron worker and small farmer as a sideline. He grew old like that, but more and more withdrawn," Baur said.

I unbuttoned my coat, stopped for a moment.

"While Cousin Berger was varying his strategies in the matter of the English inheritance, one of his brothers rode his bicycle through new snow into the village brook, where he landed with his face in a puddle of water and lay there. This place was approximately three hundred paces away from the house of Albert Baur, in whose attic the clocks were still ticking whether leaves were dancing or new snow was lying, and some four hundred paces north of the farm of Joachim Schwarz, who, when the manure pits were full, staged processions by sending his drivers out with the manure wagons to manure the egg dealer's large field, where the grasses, buttercups, daisies, crane's-bill, forget-me-nots refreshed themselves on the fragrance of this excrement, incorporated it in order to grow big and strong, blue and yellow, in the wind, toward the light.

"Then a second brother came to grief with his bicycle. He was riding down a mountain road, skidded off, crashed into a telephone pole, lay there.

"A third brother burned to death on the electric wires of the ironworks. The fourth, butcher by profession, got a cut while slaughtering, which he died from," Baur said.

A gust of wind seized my coat from behind, making it billow out, while from the Hardwald a crow was heard, and a passing car made the tails of my coat flutter violently.

"Bindschädler, I can remember how my father's sister, the mother of those cousins who fell victim to accidents, was laid out on the threshing floor of her small farm, surrounded by flowers through which a draft was blowing. And one accompanied the dead woman in a procession through the village, to the field with the huge elm.

"In his final months, by the way, Berger was confined to his bed. And when he was dead his wife became unbearable. She also got into difficulties with the neighbors," Baur said.

I thought of the parrot in the *Arakanga* pet store, and that in the meantime it must have scratched itself behind the ears with two toes of its unfettered left or fettered right foot.

Baur stuck his left hand in his pants pocket, his right in the pocket of his jacket. While we were walking along the housefronts I brought my soles down harder and louder, at least for a while.

Cars came toward us. Cars passed us. I said that one had recently heard that in spite of the economic recession car purchases had risen by ten to sixteen percent. So you could conclude that the man of today (also the woman) was striving first for a car, then for a TV, a refrigerator.

"So there it would finally be: the mobile, accessible, overcooled world: the opposite perhaps of those sketched worlds. Yes!" Baur said, setting his cap to rights, smiling.

New snow doesn't get to lie under pear trees (according to Baur), at least not when they are in the wind; so that the morning after new snow green shadows would be lying under the pear trees, under apple trees too, making the sketched world something of a colored one, I thought to myself—and that years ago I had seen a girl, a little girl with a doll, in the middle of the grounds of a school that formed an enormous square surrounding a playing field. The girl was walking along one of the façades. A leaf hopped after her. The girl noticed the leaf, talked to the leaf, the leaf lay where it was. The girl with the doll trotted on, looked back, talked to the doll. The leaf lifted up, hopped after her, overtook the girl, lay there. The girl caught up to the leaf, passed it, looked back, spoke to it. The leaf took off, rushed toward her, hopped past. The girl with the doll hopped after it, reached the leaf, stepped on it—cradled the doll.— On the stone steps a stone girl was playing the flute.—It was on that playing field, incidentally, that I first met Baur.

We were now on the gently rising Aarauerstrasse. At the moment it was cool.

"Bindschädler, the sound of your soles reminded me of our shoemaker (the baker's brother), who was a gymnast too. For a time, as top gymnast when it came to local, cantonal, or even national competition, he introduced the Amrain club's team to group exercises on the horizontal bar, the parallel bars, and the horse. He was also skilled at teaching one on one. Furthering budding or advanced gymnasts was especially close to his heart, this shoemaker and brother of the baker whose house stands as it were exposed after the property-owner's farmstead built onto it was torn down, so that the house, in this case the east front of the baker's or Linda's house, exhibited the arrangement of the rooms of the torn-down farmstead dwelling, and here and there even its baseboards or floorboards, while on the south side the pergola with the wisteria still arches over the terrace, with the same cracks today that the baker walked over when he was off to win a wreath at gymnastics, or when he returned with a beribboned wreath on his head.

"And you know, Bindschädler, back then in the bakery was where I said good-bye to Linda. It cost her some tears. I can still smell them today. And it really was a good-bye for life.

"Now we see each other occasionally at class reunions. One tells oneself that well, those were good times, those school years, we really felt good together, and one believed it would go on that way, that one could or would like to have that feeling for a long time, perhaps a lifetime. But it turned out otherwise, and her son is now in America, and she was recently there too, but America didn't appeal to her at all, those houses with air conditioners, houses where you couldn't open the windows when you wanted to, houses in which there was always a draft and the drone of air conditioners. She couldn't stand such houses, and was happy to have come back to Switzerland.

"And then you have a dance together, pro forma. Are kind and polite to each other, secretly watching the film that's screening within one, showing episodes from our young days, as a silent film, of course, accompanied in part by old songs, school and folk songs ("What the Swallow Sang" . . . and so forth).—

"So, Bindschädler, the slapping of your soles reminded me of our shoemaker, whom I once met on a glorious summer day standing in front of his workshop (the property, by the way, is still there today, with an almost baroque wrought-iron grille in front of the shop window on the south side, whose function it was to protect the precious stock of shoes from thieves, brown shoes that one bought for one's confirmation and that had a special aroma one took with one through life). Meeting him I was barefoot, which led to his remarking, 'Little boy! At the train station they are hanging barefoot boys today!' I concealed my panic and went off, still in the direction of the train station, but when I was out of sight I turned around and hurried straight home. I crossed the apple orchard of the doctor who had settled in the former post office, that is, he added a house onto it, a house with a wood bower and an enormous curved roof. I still know today, by the way, that the stucco was mixed with the color of the original façade (a darkish Imperial yellow), which proved durable, for it has lasted to the present. Today a painter lives there. The current doctor (son of the former one) built a house with an atrium next door. The house with the enormous curved roof was built at the same time as the hospital for whose bazaar Johanna was representing *Helvetia* on a horse-drawn float adorned with summer flowers.

"Years later we played at putting on a fair in the apple orchard, with games of chance, shooting galleries, and so forth. Every boy taking part had to bring along prizes for these games of chance and shooting galleries. I asked my mother for the little porcelain figures on the chest of drawers in our living room. I could have them. I went off, full of pride, full of grief too at having to part from them, perhaps forever. I won them back, the little porcelain couples, to my mother's joy too. The doctor was also among those who came. He even frequented the shooting gallery, which made the organizers happy of course," Baur said.

I thought, while Baur was now silent, of crickets. Then saw before my eyes the snow-covered fir trees, Stifter's collected, no, selected works. I asked myself again whether he had read it, Stifter's *Indian Summer*, which I always connected with the light in March, with a region without shadows, without sound. Except for the drafts caused by cars it was almost windstill. The daylight had faded noticeably. At times one saw gulls even over the Hardwald.

"A group picture still exists of the Amrain gymnastic club from the shoemaker's time, the time of the baker, Benno, and the Berger cousin who drowned in the village brook. The picture was taken in front of the brewery, under two chestnut trees, horse chestnuts, that flanked the entrance, at the same time covering the veranda. The two chestnut trees are still there today, the veranda as well, together with its wrought-iron railing.

"When I pass by it—whether in summer, winter, or even in November, when only a few leaves are hanging in the immediate vicinity of the streetlight, which is strange, but you see it again and again, I recently encountered it again in Basel, near the cathedral, where practically all the chestnut trees were leafless, it was only around a streetlight that the branches still bore them, in full strength so to speak and wonderfully colored, of course, as if they felt themselves to be children of the light—when I pass by these chestnuts in front of the brewery I occasionally think I have been transported back to that moment when I, some seven paces northeast of the trunk of the northernmost chestnut, was waiting for the parade, and where Johanna as *Helvetia* glided past high above me, surrounded by glorious summer flowers.

"Since then the gymnastics club has presumably gotten another banner. And of the people in the group picture two, three, are still alive, who, by the way, were kneeling in front. Most of the champion gymnasts were standing in the back row, near the banner held by standard-bearer Berger, who was later to lie with his face in a puddle in new snow and night.

"This group picture with banner spent years in the attic, behind a bedspring. I fetched it down and gave it to one of our daughters. Now it hangs above her desk, has a light brownish cast, even shimmers like mother of pearl, at least from certain angles, is about fifty by seventy centimeters, behind glass, in a brown frame," Baur said, turning away a little, taking a deep breath.

I buttoned my coat.

"Bindschädler, in most cases the graves of those gymnasts in the cemetery in Amrain have already been cleared away.

"There too, by the way, stood the gravestone of Linda's mother. She died, I believe, giving birth to Linda. The stone was of white marble, showing at the very top a relief, a high relief, representing an angel staring diagonally downward into the earth of the cemetery, a bouquet of lilies on its arm.

"There was another grave there with a similar tombstone, only its figure had no wings. A bronze urn stood at the foot end of this grave. The wife was lying in the earth. The ashes of the husband were in the bronze urn. The wife died by gas. The husband (as a former Cavalry Major) by pistol."

In the sky clouds drifted by, exposing pink-colored patches.

"Over the course of time the Cavalry Major's urn began to leak, that is, the ashes began to run out at the bottom, in part sticking to the bronze, so that it had to strike one that the ashes of the Cavalry Major were now taking flight, blown away by the wind.

"Bindschädler, whenever I was at the cemetery in Amrain I always walked by this grave and tidied the base of the urn, and the stone as well of course, whose angel had a white rose instead of lilies, and no wings. The Cavalry Major's family played a certain role in Johanna's life, in that Johanna did her apprenticeship as a sales clerk in the store of the agricultural cooperative across the street and then worked there for years as a sales clerk, and was occasionally a guest of the family of the Cavalry Major.

"So in that part of the town there were Alfred Baur, whose clocks ticked away Amrain time; the farmer, butcher, and cattle dealer Joachim Schwarz, who sent out his drivers when it was time to manure the big field, and whose apple orchard produced magnificent forget-me-nots; and here too—adjoining the agricultural property of Joachim Schwarz—was the farm of the Cavalry Major, who, like his father before him, had been for years head of the local council; then came the elementary school and across the way the cooperative store.

"Not far away, near the final resting place of the Cavalry Major and his wife, is that of my cousin Johann, the last tramp in our part of the country. In autumn, when the weather is fine, and if I happen to be there, I stop at this place and report: 'Johann, it is autumn on earth!' Bindschädler, Amrain is a carpet, if not a Persian one still a carpet with motifs. The motifs are the generations, the clans, the families. The warp is the landscape, the woof is time. Some of the motifs are fresh and shining, others appear somewhat worn, still others threadbare, furthermore there are places where only the warp is visible. Yes!" Baur said.

In the gardens, pear trees shone when the light hit them. Baur stopped, bent over, checked his shoelaces, retied them, stood up, smiled at me, put his cap straight, and again walked on.

"The wife of the Cavalry Major was the sawmill owner's daughter, while her brother was Anna's brother-in-law. Anna, as you know, had been seized under the cherry trees, two of which are still standing, in the garden of a one-family house, because Anna's property together with the adjoining land had been sold off at the first opportunity by her brother-in-law, the brother of the Cavalry Major's wife, the adjoining land becoming a large construction site that became a garden quarter.

"The two cherry trees are those that appear as gossamer forms in watercolor against dark mauve, as long as one takes the time, in fine weather, on the west side of the property, to attend the coming of the November evening. Under the rearmost cherry tree, which today flanks the entrance to a one-family house, is where Anna was seized. Afterward, Anna came back once, one morning, in a nightgown, but without staying.

"So Anna, our neighbor, was the sister of the sister-in-law of the wife of the Cavalry Major whose urn leaked and whose former farmstead presented a west wall, which—with its partly flaking stucco, its colorations—bears some resemblance to the paintings or artworks of Tapies, the Spanish artist, who made them by removing parts from such walls, or which could be copies of certain parts of the wall surfaces of properties that in his time at least might have been inhabited by Cavalry Majors who would have put an end to their careers with their officer's pistols, and whose wives before them, with the help of gas, would have condescended to find themselves ready to prepare an ending to their memoirs.

"Bindschädler, long-stemmed autumn daisies bloom against this quite unusual wall of the farmstead that was later taken over by Joachim Schwarz, after the generation of the Cavalry Major was gone. I don't know what their real names were. And it can happen that in the burning summer sun the bushes wither, so that one fears that this Tapies painting must exist henceforth without the yellow autumn daisies. But then it happens again and again (at least over the course of years it always did) that they are able to pick themselves up and flower in late Indian summer to ornament this same west wall, whose upper part is protected by an overhang of tiles and whose lower half has been replaced with zinc-covered metal, presumably on account of the wind, which is fond of catching on such overhangs. The metal sheath acquired in time a coating of rust, giving the west wall of the farmstead a rather repulsive streaking; on the other hand, a zinc-metal surface discolored by rust can be fascinating.

"So the farmstead was later taken over by Joachim Schwarz after the Cavalry Major's clan was gone. Joachim Schwarz left the farmstead to one of his sons, who in the course of time, however, became one of the great host of those who were treated by my father, among others, and who are still sheltered today in the Burghölzli clinic, in St. Urban, in Bellelay, in the Rosegg, the Waldau, year after year, in order in the end to give them over to the earth, thinking that one has done one's duty.

"The south side of this property too has a wisteria pergola, but here climbing roses have been added that have reverted to wild ones, so that in early summer in the middle of the village, in this quite particular part, wild roses bloom as they bloom at forest edges or in hedges, insofar as there still are any," Baur said.

I thought of the little house in the Ulica Dabrowiecka that contains a collection of seven thousand artworks, thought particularly of Jozef Lurka's *Eve with Trout in Paradise*, in which Lurka wanted to indicate what was paradisiacal about this paradise, for where, since the Fall of Man, has a trout ever let itself be stroked?

"In the village, Bindschädler, one also gets to see what happens to faces, what life or time has done with the faces one has known from childhood on. It's hard to distinguish between sympathetic and unsympathetic, beautiful and ugly, clever and stupid faces. Rather, you ask yourself: 'What has time, what has life done with these faces?'

"The same thing happens with houses. What doesn't time do to those? It makes me think of the property of a gymnast who spent his life as an independent bicycle mechanic, from whom at the time I did *not* buy my bicycle. This house has a rough stucco that had originally been painted bright red, a wooden arbor, and also an almost baroque wrought-iron grille in front of the window of the cellar workshop. Bindschädler, how the red darkened, the wood of the arbor lost its color, as the property aged along with the aging of the gymnast, and then when he was dead it disintegrated rapidly, although it went on being lived in—to observe that, Bindschädler, was deeply moving.

"North of this property the mountain with the little woods in front begins, in which in the spring anemones bloom, everlasting, woodruff, then enchanter's nightshade," Baur said, nervously fiddling with his cap.

I compared Baur's face with the one I saw for the first time on the aforementioned playing field surrounded by schoolhouses, where the girl with the doll performed her ballet with the leaf to music piped by a girl of stone.

I became aware that this same flutist must have accompanied the changes in Baur's face, the night marches as well, where the shooting stars passed over the single-file column; before they disappeared one did not, yet again, find time—to express wishes. The girl on the steps must have gone on blowing her flute too while Ferdinand was cooking trees, Philipp painting the country house, Schwarz's drivers transporting manure, and while flower petals sailed over Lina's funeral procession, ahead at the bend in the road; to say nothing of the three women with winter asters, at whose appearance cherry trees presented themselves as torches, occasionally circled around by crows (freely after Baur).

Here and there a rose was still blooming. There were nasturtiums in the gardens, but above all winter asters, in white (shot through with soft pink), red, mauve.

Some chrysanthemums, golden, copper-colored, were arranged here and there on steps. One could make out the places where snowdrops would blossom in the spring, and anemones. Also the location of crocuses seemed to be calling for attention.

I thought of Schönbrunn, its park, its almost mystical beech dungeons with roses inside, statues in hedge niches; saw its plumes of dust that condescend to occur or twirl in March and August; remembered the flowering time of the allées of chestnut trees, and that that is when petals sail down onto the shoulders of passersby.

I said to myself that people tried again and again to live with gardens, and that the Chinese are even said to associate gardens with happiness.

Sissi, the Empress Elisabeth, came to mind, and how she wandered through the world and died in Geneva, by chance, and how the Kaiser took leave of her in the Burgkapelle, where he had previously bade farewell to his son. And I found that *Mayerling* almost came close to *Arakanga*, at least in sound; and the Vienna Woods arose before my eyes, the cemetery of Pötzleinsdorf in which candles burn at night; felt the excitement that took hold of me when I turned into the Ringstrasse in Vienna for the first time, at the streetcar stop near the university; saw the monumental figures before me, those riders and steeds and eagles on rooftops (officious structures, of course); remembered the Mozart monument, and that Gottfried Semper had a role in working on the staffage of the Ringstrasse; skipped in thought to Baden bei Wien outside Vienna, strode through its sanitarium gardens, which today are as they were in the Kaiser's time, with white chairs beneath the chestnut trees, in the hedge niches poets, thinkers, and Haydn; saw the Imperial yellow on the house façades of Baden bei Wien.

Two, three gulls flew away above us. Now and then a crow cawed over from the Hardwald.

"Bindschädler, we do not live in order to be always pocketing or handing out lessons. This constant intense chattering is the kind that crows do when they caw, where the sounds must, so to speak, be extruded from the stomach in a wavy line, so that the changing location of the expected sound on the body's contours can be communicated," Baur said abruptly, as if he had remembered *The Word for a New Day*, which is broadcast on workdays at quarter to seven.

Cars were driving toward the east, toward the west. The draft from them grabbed one's coat just as one stopped to unbutton it, reminding one of the performance of the heart (twelve thousand liters a day, eighteen thousand tank trucks over a lifetime). One told oneself that most people who have a first heart attack don't die of it.

"Opposite the former property of Joachim Schwarz is a restaurant where the funeral meal after the burial of school friends, male and female, takes place. You eat your plate of meats (salami, ham, mortadella), your piece of bread, drink a glass of red wine. In most cases one chats about this or that. One thinks that the salami, the ham, the mortadella, has cost one or several animals their lives," Baur said.

Clouds were again drifting across the sky as if they were scabs that had broken off from an enormous wound.

"Bindschädler, the next day part of this funeral meal flows beyond this restaurant in the sewer pipes to arrive at the sewage treatment plant, then from there into the canal, from the canal into the Dünnern, then in Olten into the Aare, from the Aare into the Rhine, from the Rhine into the sea, from which the sun, as one is accustomed to saying, draws water up again, wraps it up in clouds that the wind drives across the continents, where as it goes it gives up the water drawn up from sewage treatment plants, mountain brooks, springs, and condensation to the mountains, brooks, rivers, of course to those fields as well that were tended by Joachim Schwarz and on which forget-me-nots thrive, large-flowered, very blue, which might be an illusion, an illusion of memory, since I don't believe that there are any particularly large-flowered forget-me-nots, as far as I have observed in all my years of being around forget-me-nots. Our blood too has its circulation, Bindschädler. Even thoughts circulate until they pass into the light, the aforementioned great light. Yes!" Baur said, slowly lifting the heel of his right foot (in place) setting it down, raising it and so forth, with an expression as if listening.

I saw the Dünnern in my mind, how it flows past the grove of plane trees near where it empties into the Aare. I thought of Bartók's *Concerto for Orchestra*, of the ballet of the plane trees, of the tennis game without a ball.

"Do you still remember, Bindschädler, how I always had to control myself when I was standing behind you after we marched to the mustering ground loaded down with all our gear, how I always had to check myself not to burst out laughing? For on the mustering ground a wave motion would go through your body from top to bottom, which might have had something to do with your height and the weight on your back. It always took a long time until Private Bindschädler was standing in the proper mustering position, that is, motionless.

"And do you still recall how, after moving out, the column stumbled into clouds that made it hard to enrich one's lungs as usual, on account of certain fumes that had been called upon to materialize, in consequence of the culinary excesses (modest, to be sure) of the evening before?" Baur said.

I thought of swarms of gulls, which in late autumn abandon now the rivers, now the lakes, briefly, of course, to fall upon freshly plowed fields in the interior (insofar as the countryside beyond the rivers, the lakes, can be so characterized). Thought of the enormous swarms of swallows, which, when the grain is ripening in southern Sweden, fly low over boundless fields of wheat, while the land is filled with light. And one thinks one hears the snapping of beaks, for they are chasing small insects, these swallows, which leads to their always snapping their beaks open and shut. And I thought that it was precisely in Sweden, southern Sweden, that the colors of the flowers, the blue of the cornflower for example, the white of the potato blossoms, are more intense than they are here with us. Remembered that there, in southern Sweden, there is chervil, which here we call giant chervil and which also grew in the *Wild West*, above all along railroad embankments, where in those days men shot at buffalos from trains while the Indians looked on from an appropriate distance, armed with bows and arrows. And I saw the local train that passed by two, three times a day at a leisurely tempo, along an embankment that could use some work, its locomotive emitting whistles in such a way that one really felt this conveyance was a *land boat*.

Meanwhile we were again walking toward the center of town. In the western sky pink had already mixed with mauve. One saw the smoke rising from the tall chimneys of the Olten-Hammer cement works. The smoke blended into the colors of the clouds, was tinged with pink, with mauve, which of course carried over to the silhouettes as well.

"It was one's first confrontation in person with classical civilization, our vacation on Kos. It was a strange sensation, tracing the ornamentation of the head of a column with one's middle finger. And then there was the light, the Aegean light. We wandered through fields of ruins, looked at mosaics, strolled through the remains of the dwelling of a goddess of love, whose walls were decorated with paintings, encountering hardly a lizard or a cicada, at most a butterfly, which moreover seemed to be flying backward. In classical times people lived with stone, above all with marble. So the people of those times were, so to speak, children of stone and of light, although they too consumed funeral meals and had to endure headaches. For even in those times the right to happiness, the right to a headache-free life, was a meager utopia.—Have you heard cicadas, Bindschädler? Evenings at eight they suddenly start up with their lunatic chirping, on the edge of the fields of ruins, in oleander bushes, pines, Persian lilacs, cypresses. It seems as if a trembling goes through the few columns still standing, which have presumably been set upright again.

"Beside the fields of ruins there are also Greek Orthodox chapels, with cupolas that have a special patina. This patina and the pines and the stones and the mauve-blooming hedges, the oleander flowers, produce a harmony, especially when the evening light falls on them, which then combines with the lunatic chirping at eight.—And then one sees couples in love strolling silently through the ruins. Greek music sounds from the loudspeakers of the tavernas where people are getting ready to have dinner. The evening light builds up on the surrounding housefronts. A boat shouts over from the harbor. The vivid Hawaii flowers bloom quietly. Freedom Square has its flâneurs. The bicycle riders work their pedals. The people beneath the loudspeakers eat bread with a spread of yogurt mixed with cucumber and garlic. The cupolas of the chapels are the musical scores of light! Yes!

"And there is always this seafarer wind (three days stronger, three days weaker). And when one, as mentioned, goes out on the sea, burly men move to the railing while children throw up in paper cups, lying on their mothers' laps. And one thinks of Odysseus, of Ithaca, of Böcklin's *Isle of the Dead*. And the space all around is the space of a thousand years, in blue and opal colors, filled with the chirping of cicadas, the murmuring of old women," Baur said, at the moment looking around as if he were surprised to find himself on the Martin-Disteli-Strasse, walking toward downtown.

"Bindschädler, to come back to Amrain: that's how the procession moved, Joachim Schwarz's manure procession, in precisely the opposite direction from the flow of today's excrement into the main channel of the sewer that passes by the restaurant, beneath the street over which Joachim Schwarz dispatched his manure drivers in the direction of the large field, while the excrement was heading south in the direction of the treatment plant, from which the purified waters went into a canal that was in part ruler straight, which emptied into the Dünnern, which in Olten led to the Aare, then to the Rhine, then in time to the ocean from which the sun sucked up water from which clouds developed, which the wind, even if it's not the wind of the Aegean, drives across the continents," Baur said, "where the clouds deposit their water again so the vines can grow, the forget-me-nots, the lilies, the cabbage, and the grain over which in high summer in southern Sweden enormous swarms of swallows can somersault above grain fields of unimaginable extent, snapping their beaks open and shut, spreading a subtle noise across the distances of this landscape from one side to the other."

(And then the chicory blooms quite particularly blue, there in Sweden, and the chervil become particularly large, I added.)

Our landscape now appeared as a watercolor, so to speak, in which the cement works of Olten-Hammer formed a central focus, if one can speak of central foci in connection with watercolors, those meager phenomena. The streaming smoke from the chimneys contributed to the constant shifting of at least the horizon of this picture. One thought of Louis Moilliet, the great watercolorist, who on August 24, 1962, while the Swiss Pavilion at the 31st Venice Biennale presented a magnificent, unfortunately much-too-late exhibition of his works that met with an enthusiastic reception, laid down paint and brush forever (as one is accustomed to put it in such cases).

"A white whale was once supposed to have wandered into the Rhine, and it was quarreled over for centuries, this or that generation having found it necessary to sanctify the river. But the Rhine is a river like other rivers, which gathers its waters from its source, carries them to the sea, and leaves them to the ocean, without the ocean getting any fuller," Baur said, while our nearer surroundings too began to fit into the great watercolor.

"It can happen, Bindschädler, if one is sitting at a funeral meal in a restaurant, that on the wall of posters on the other side of the brook—which can no longer be seen, it's covered by a sidewalk—(and beneath the street, as mentioned, there is the main line of the sewer pipe through which the sewage and the excrement are flowing in the direction opposite that which the manure processions of Joachim Schwarz were pleased to take when it was a matter of manuring the egg dealer's large field) that on the wall of posters beyond the sidewalk spots of color appear, whose connections or significance are not to be made out through the curtains; it's a question of spots of mauve, violet, white, and red tones that now begin to sound, like (let's say) those musical scores in color of the Greek Orthodox chapels at the edge of ancient fields of ruins, so that the only things really still missing are the cicadas and the wind of the Aegean.—Instead, one has in the restaurant the showcases containing trophies, mementos of soccer-club victories. A banner too is hanging, if one remembers rightly, in one of the showcases.

"And then one conjures up Joachim Schwarz as he stood on the bridge opposite (which is no longer there) in his butcher's apron, a corner pinned up, inspecting the parade of manure wagons taking away excrement in the direction opposite today's river of sewage. And one conjures up as well the egg dealer, massive, with heavy stride (almost a duck's waddle), his basket of eggs on his left arm, on his way to the train station to take the local train to the weekly market of the town boasting the playing field I mentioned, at whose edge a stone girl is playing the flute, and from which he returned again in the course of the afternoon, perhaps in time to attend the parade of the manure wagons orchestrated by Joachim Schwarz," Baur said.

I had to think of Ravel's *Bolero*, of how this piece of music begins softly, incorporates more and more elements, keeping the original ones, grows, almost overflows . . .

Meanwhile it had become cooler.

"Of course I had not only male cousins, but female ones too," Baur said.

At that moment I was seeing the heating niche where the Holy Family coexisted, carved in wood, with Lenin and the Last Supper beneath the radiator, and thought of how the little house on the Ulica Dabrowiecka had for a long time not been a residence with a private collection inside but a full-blown museum, in which, astonishingly, a family was still living, making do with the space left for it by some seven thousand works of art that had conquered every corner, even the pantry and toilet.

"Bindschädler, Böcklin painted five versions of *Isle of the Dead*. And there are something like five continents, if you consider Asia and Europe as one (which is essentially the case) and exclude the Arctic, since it is in any event uninhabited. In the catalog these five versions are listed under a single number, so that it seems there is only one version of *Isle of the Dead*. I was recently in the art museum in Basel, by the way, and sought out Böcklin's *Isle of the Dead*. A man in a black cape was already standing there. I went away. Came back later. The man was still there. I went away again. Came back once more. The situation hadn't changed. I gave up.

"The *Isle of the Dead* was said to be hanging in rooms in countless reproductions around the turn of the century, in the fin de siècle," Baur said.

To which I replied that in 1951 Georg Schmidt gave a lecture on Böcklin, really a scholar's summing up of the painter. But Schmidt characterized the *Isle of the Dead*, the *Sacred Grove*, *Painting and Poetry*, and many other works as *commonplaces*, whereas in his opinion the *Children Carving May Flutes* belonged artistically and humanly to Böcklin's happiest inspiration. "The coming to terms with the impressive power of Impressionism," as Wölfflin says, had not at that time conclusively taken hold. But motifs like the isle of the dead had, on the other hand, since the first decades of the twentieth century, already been adopted by the Surrealists. Giorgio de Chirico and Dalì refer to Böcklin not only in their paintings but in their writings as well. Furthermore, Dalì placed the Swiss artist in the great tradition of fantastic painting. Already in 1920, de Chirico championed him in an essay. Today Arnold Böcklin is regarded by many as one of the greatest artistic personalities from the end of the nineteenth century.

The cowpats in the sky were moving calmly eastward. The colors in the west became increasingly intense. The smoke from the chimneys of the Olten-Hammer cement works continued to blend with them. The humming of cars swelled, diminished.

I thought of crickets' carrying their ears in their front legs, visible on a shining silver eardrum, and that these organs of hearing excluded the songs of other species, functioning as a *filter*. But as for the *arbitrator* that distinguishes between species-specific and species-antithetic songs, researchers have not yet tracked down its location. They suspect it is in the brain. They have succeeded in discovering in the brain two omega cells that steer the sounds crickets receive like a sound compass, with whose aid the female crickets find their way to the calling males.

"Bindschädler, I didn't know my female cousins well. But one especially has stayed in my memory: Lisa, fine-limbed, who always went to church dressed in white (summers at least), carrying white gloves and wearing a straw hat with artificial cherries. Lisa was a trained seamstress. She was also talented at embroidery. *Job 25* was inscribed on her mother's tombstone; the grave, inside a beech hedge, always displayed three geraniums, rank ones. And her clan lived in the house of my father's father! I had female cousins from whom one heard nothing for decades, only to find out long after they were dead that their daughters, at least in one case, had got involved with showmen. Then one imagined how this cousin with her showmen lived in an apartment in the barracks quarter, from which they would depart to travel the fairs with their shooting galleries, for example, a merry-go-round, a boat swing. One remembered that cousin Elise (not Aunt Elise) had also traveled the fairs. And one always had Stravinsky's *Petrushka* in mind, for I believe that Russia and fairs, honky-tonk and dancing bears, go together.

"Once, another cousin, the aunt of the one who traveled the fairs, as she was passing through Amrain, pulled down the window of her train car to greet us smiling, we happened to be at the train station by chance. But she also let her glance pass over the area, first of course over the station grounds, on whose square Benno had once practiced marching and gymnastic exercises with the gymnastics club for a national competition, and which he, Benno, remembered thirty-five years later when, eighteen hours before his death, as he was standing in front of his isolated house at five A.M. in pajamas, in boots, a cup of coffee in his hand.

And one had at that moment the feeling that this cousin had lived only in order to pull down the train window at breast height as she passed through Amrain, her hands on the window pulls, her arms outspread. One thought of painting on the back of glass, and that this process has existed for some two thousand years, that it was especially widespread in the baroque era, and that in the nineteenth century it was mass produced but was always original work done by hand. Probably the most famous painter on glass today lives in a small Croatian village near the Hungarian border, in Hlebine, his name is Ivan Generalić.

"So this cousin's nieces probably spent their evenings sitting in the kitchen before those great nights that are followed by days full of honky-tonk, frippery. And when it is late, that is late in the year, the hydrangeas down in the garden rustle, for there have been hydrangeas around barracks quarters for quite some time, while in the past they would have been found more frequently around castles, around Eulenberg Castle, for example, on the other side of Lake Constance.

"And soldiers are still sitting around in these barracks quarters today, evenings of course, as the Ulans did in the Kaiser's time. Occasionally one produces a harmonica, even plays an accordion. And then something like the wind from a Russian fair blows through the sparse grass of the exercise fields, and boats sail across the sky, borne by colorful balloons," Baur said, shoving his cap back and sticking his hands in the accustomed pockets.

I saw in my mind the old hospital on the Fahrweg, about which Baur said that it always reminded him of Tolstoy's Yasnaya Polyana, although their architecture has nothing in common. Presumably it's only the atmosphere of the park and the shimmering-through of the façades that enabled Baur to evoke Yasnaya Polyana. But I also saw before me bushes of holly with their red berries whose branches were hoarded for a period, usually before Christmas. Today holly with red berries is scarcely still to be found in the woods of the Jura.

I continued further in my thoughts to the bust of Nicolaus Riggenbach, who had endowed the aforementioned weather column on which is inscribed that he, Riggenbach, was born in Guebweiler on May 21, 1817, attended school in Basel, did his mechanic's apprenticeship in Lyon and Paris and so forth, and was finally called to Olten as head of the Swiss National Railways workshop before which steam locomotive 2958 stands even today, a product of the Winterthur Swiss Locomotive and Machine Factory. Nicolaus Riggenbach stares into the city park as if trying to make out a train with a steam locomotive. The trees of the city park seem conscious of their significance: summers to dispense shade, good air, winters to simulate watercolor beings watercolored on the evening sky.

A light gust of wind sent a larger swarm of leaves toward us, which was, however, intercepted by a car passing us from behind. The swarm was caught up in a spiral motion, out of which it absorbed the car's pursuit, so to speak.

"Bindschädler, recently I again remembered that when I was passing the two chestnut trees in front of the brewery between or in front of which the gymnasts had arranged themselves for a group picture at the time (the back row standing, the banner in its center, the middle row sitting, the front row kneeling, the rows slightly wavy) that I must have been standing about seven paces away from the chestnut tree to the north, in a northeasterly direction, when the parade passed by in which Johanna represented the Mother of Our Country.

"The parade's route was also, in part, the route Joachim Schwarz's drivers took when they drove with four, five special manure wagons through the village to manure the large field in whose apple orchard forget-me-nots blossomed the like of which I have not seen since. Today the main sewer pipe runs under this street, with the excrement flowing in the opposite direction. So it can happen that after a funeral meal in the restaurant mentioned, the next day those plates of meat, that is to say their excremental salami, ham, mortadella, pass beyond this restaurant, beneath the wall with posters that one used to observe and which showed blue, red, and mauve tones that brought to mind the cupolas of Greek Orthodox chapels at the edge of ancient fields of ruins, so that, as it were, a seafarer's wind was again blowing through one and through the chirping of the cicadas, while one conjured up the image of the ferryman to Hell conducting one to the island of the children of light," Baur said.

From the towers of the city it struck four.

At that moment we were walking past an art nouveau house, upon which I said to Baur that in spite of its revolutionary manifestos art nouveau did not abandon the artificial paradises of the end of the century; its consciousness of spring awakening remained shot through with the heavy dreams of the past. Its celebration of life remained in a secret, uncanny relation to sympathy with death. Inversely, the fin de siècle showed tendencies that pointed forward. One had to think of the ambiguity of Nietzsche's philosophy, in which art nouveau and fin de siècle mingled. For Nietzsche said that he had a finer nose for signs of beginning and decline than any man had ever had; he was the teacher of this par excellence. He knew both. He was both.

Baur stopped, lifted his left pant leg, regarded his shoe, dropped his pant leg, walked on.

I said further that Otto Julius Bierbaum said that Paradise had been taken away from man and man gave himself art instead. And that there was no morality in Paradise, and that art was Paradise reclaimed.

Art, here proclaimed as conquest and program, appears in Count Kessler's writing only in the context of our irreparable separation from vegetative life. There is no longer any talk of art. Over time its will to beauty could not fend off the droning of the industrial age, had not been able to surmount the bitterness and ugliness of mortal existence, had not been able to deify man. Representations of political salvation had usurped the place of belief in the aesthetic transformation of the human race, had also, to be sure, mingled with it. The idea of salvation had run through the nineteenth century, and experienced in the fin de siècle and in art nouveau an intensification to the point of obsession. Our time too is possessed by a striving for salvation, and this is one of the reasons our own era finds the fin de siècle so attractive.

The sun was sitting as a gigantic disk of red gold on the silhouette of the cement works, so that the smoke from its chimneys profited from this red gold. It appeared as if snow was to be expected shortly. I had in my ear the ticking of the quartz clock that hangs in our kitchen, as they are accustomed to hang in kitchens, these square quartz clocks from the Migros stores, fifty francs each. It is quite true, as you are told when buying them, that these clocks gain or lose only a minute a year. Indeed! What more do you want? The clockmaker with his shop around the corner doesn't like this sort of thing. But apparently that's the way it goes. One wants to buy in the milling crowd where one can buy everything at once, where one can *take* it and only has to pay the cashier, and then what does it matter what one pays so long as one was able to *take* it, while at the same time all around one as many people as possible have also been *taking*, piling things into carts. And this faint, placid ticking brought to mind a grandfather clock in a parsonage, where a painting was said to be hanging on the wall, representing a girl in a blue-green damask dress, a gold chain around her body, on her head an ornament of gold and silver sequins, holding a dead child's skull and a white rose. But every time, the *Girl on Red Ground* would intrude on this picture (according to Baur).

From time to time, as long as my eyes could stand it, I watched the sinking sun. Baur was walking beside me as if he was not aware of anything. The snow clouds were steadily approaching from the northwest. The pink and opal spots on the sidewalk were occurring again, more frequently. Now and then a gull flew over the landscape. Above the edge of the woods crows were lamenting, fighting over their night quarters.

"Bindschädler, there's one cousin I haven't told you anything about. Her name was Ida, she was the sister of the Lisa I mentioned (called Lisel), the sister of Mina too, so that in that family there was an Ida, a Lise, a Mina. They had a brother named Werner. He was for years a court official in Amrain. Alongside that he was a small farmer, wore a moustache like that of his cousin Alfred Baur, who pedaled on his special bicycle through the village, the stump of his cigar pointing diagonally upward beneath his moustache. Cousin Ida's husband came from a leaseholder family. He worked in a stone quarry business, which gave him pneumoconiosis. He became thinner and thinner, paler too, and died from this disease. When Rudolf (Ida's husband) died, I helped get him out of the house. Helped him be carried down, down an extremely steep wooden staircase. Of course Rudolf with his pneumoconiosis lay in his coffin. Someone had to support me from behind so we could make it down safely. And Rudolf was deposited, that is, the coffin with Rudolf inside, in the hearse, while the mourners were standing on the west side of the farmstead. One heard the creek pouring into the fire pond.

"Birches stood on the south side of the fire pond, in a line. We had met earlier from time to time, Linda and I, beneath the last of these birches, as it was getting dark and only briefly. Later, whenever I saw these birches, I always saw Linda there too.

"After Rudolf died of pneumoconiosis Cousin Ida left Amrain, went to a daughter who had married a farmer with whom she ran a farm in the foothills of the Alps. After the death of Werner, the court official, Lisa and Mina too moved to the foothills of the Alps.

"One day Ida arrived from the foothills of the Alps. My wife and I were eating lunch. We heard someone running the well pump. We looked out, discovered Cousin Ida. Ida was washing at the well. We called hello. Ida said she had to wash her skirt. To which we said, but you are wearing your skirt. Ida said, this morning she had had a premonition, that is why she put on two skirts. And indeed, she had fallen in the narrow Bahnhofstrasse after she had turned around to look at a man. But she hadn't hurt herself. And she had been looking forward for a long time to coming to Amrain for a few days. And now she had been able to arrange it. (Lisa and Mina were dead.) And now she was going to stay with us for a few days. And she hoped it wouldn't be a bother. And she had brought along her pills. She had trouble with her digestion and so forth. So she always had to have these pills at hand. But it was all homeopathic stuff. Completely harmless. Made from herbs.

"Days later and as a parting gift, Cousin Ida wanted to have a small basket of cherries, of the best sort. It was Ida's last visit.

"Lisa, as already mentioned, had died earlier, of homesickness. Lisa was buried in the foothills of the Alps. Lisa would definitely have liked to have *Job 25* inscribed in the vicinity of her cross. My cousins were figures from Job anyway. But they also resembled little Meret, who was *immortalized* in a damask dress whose hem (forming a large circle) concealed her feet," Baur said.

I looked at the western sky. The disk had disappeared, the red gold remained. The snow clouds had meanwhile drawn closer. Twilight rose out of the east.

"Bindschädler, at the back of our orchard we have little daffodils. When they are beginning to bloom I crouch down, say 'hello,' and wait for a light gust of wind. As boys Philipp and I used to bring back the bulbs of these daffodils from up on the mountain, in the Löwen Valley. While we were digging up the bulbs a voice rang out from a nearby bush: 'Stop! Or I'll shoot!' Without letting go of our booty we ran home. It later turned out that a hunter had been making fun of us. We planted the daffodils northeast of the cherry tree at the sight of which brother-in-law Ferdinand said: 'I no longer let any of my cherry trees get so tall. I saw them all off on top. I don't want any more tall cherry trees.'—

"So as soon as there is a white shimmer at the back of the orchard in the spring I go there, crouch down, listen—and then I really hear the daffodils ringing out over the landscape," Baur said, with, at the moment, his left hand in his pants pocket, his right stuck in his jacket pocket.

"Picasso is said to have once remarked to Malraux that you had to tear people out of their sleep, shake up the way they identify things, from the ground up. Had to create unacceptable pictures, make them fume. One must force them to see that they live in a crazy world. A world without security, a world that is not the way they thought it was."

The twilight had in the meantime progressed.

"Bindschädler, if I should ever get around to writing, I want to do it Picasso's way."

It was now beginning to snow.

SWISS LITERATURE SERIES

In 2008, Pro Helvetia, the Swiss Arts Council, began working with
Dalkey Archive Press to identify some of the greatest and most
innovative authors in twentieth and twenty-first century Swiss
letters, in the tradition of such world renowned writers as Max
Frisch, Robert Walser, and Robert Pinget. Dalkey Archive editors
met with critics and scholars in Zurich, Geneva, Basel, and Bern,
and went on to prepare reports on numerous important Swiss
authors whose work was deemed underrepresented in English.
Developing from this ongoing collaboration, the Swiss Literature
Series, launched in 2011 with Gerhard Meier's *Isle of the Dead* and
Aglaja Veteranyi's *Why the Child Is Cooking in the Polenta*, will
begin remedying this dearth of Swiss writing in the Anglophone
world with a bold initiative to publish four titles a year, each sup-
plemented with marketing efforts far exceeding what publishers
can normally provide for works in translation.

With works originating from German, French, Italian, and
Rhaeto-Romanic, the Swiss Literature Series will stand as a testi-
mony to Switzerland's contribution to world literature.

GERHARD MEIER was born in 1917. Spending six months in a sanatorium for tuberculosis made him decide to leave his job at a lamp factory and devote himself exclusively to writing. He produced a steady stream of poetry and fiction thereafter, dying in 2008 at the age of 91.

BURTON PIKE is Professor Emeritus of Comparative Literature and German at CUNY. He co-translated Musil's *The Man without Qualities*, and has translated Goethe's *The Sorrows of Young Werther* and Rilke's novel *The Notebooks of Malte Laurids Brigge*. His translations have appeared in numerous periodicals.

SELECTED DALKEY ARCHIVE PAPERBACKS

PETROS ABATZOGLOU, *What Does Mrs. Freeman Want?*
MICHAL AJVAZ, *The Golden Age.*
The Other City.
PIERRE ALBERT-BIROT, *Grabinoulor.*
YUZ ALESHKOVSKY, *Kangaroo.*
FELIPE ALFAU, *Chromos.*
Locos.
JOÃO ALMINO, *The Book of Emotions.*
IVAN ÂNGELO, *The Celebration.*
The Tower of Glass.
DAVID ANTIN, *Talking.*
ANTÓNIO LOBO ANTUNES,
Knowledge of Hell.
The Splendor of Portugal.
ALAIN ARIAS-MISSON, *Theatre of Incest.*
IFTIKHAR ARIF AND WAQAS KHWAJA, EDS.,
Modern Poetry of Pakistan.
JOHN ASHBERY AND JAMES SCHUYLER,
A Nest of Ninnies.
ROBERT ASHLEY, *Perfect Lives.*
GABRIELA AVIGUR-ROTEM, *Heatwave and Crazy Birds.*
HEIMRAD BÄCKER, *transcript.*
DJUNA BARNES, *Ladies Almanack.*
Ryder.
JOHN BARTH, *LETTERS.*
Sabbatical.
DONALD BARTHELME, *The King.*
Paradise.
SVETISLAV BASARA, *Chinese Letter.*
RENÉ BELLETTO, *Dying.*
MARK BINELLI, *Sacco and Vanzetti Must Die!*
ANDREI BITOV, *Pushkin House.*
ANDREJ BLATNIK, *You Do Understand.*
LOUIS PAUL BOON, *Chapel Road.*
My Little War.
Summer in Termuren.
ROGER BOYLAN, *Killoyle.*
IGNÁCIO DE LOYOLA BRANDÃO,
Anonymous Celebrity.
The Good-Bye Angel.
Teeth under the Sun.
Zero.
BONNIE BREMSER,
Troia: Mexican Memoirs.
CHRISTINE BROOKE-ROSE, *Amalgamemnon.*
BRIGID BROPHY, *In Transit.*
MEREDITH BROSNAN, *Mr. Dynamite.*
GERALD L. BRUNS, *Modern Poetry and the Idea of Language.*
EVGENY BUNIMOVICH AND J. KATES, EDS.,
Contemporary Russian Poetry: An Anthology.
GABRIELLE BURTON, *Heartbreak Hotel.*
MICHEL BUTOR, *Degrees.*
Mobile.
Portrait of the Artist as a Young Ape.
G. CABRERA INFANTE, *Infante's Inferno.*
Three Trapped Tigers.
JULIETA CAMPOS,
The Fear of Losing Eurydice.
ANNE CARSON, *Eros the Bittersweet.*
ORLY CASTEL-BLOOM, *Dolly City.*
CAMILO JOSÉ CELA, *Christ versus Arizona.*
The Family of Pascual Duarte.
The Hive.
LOUIS-FERDINAND CÉLINE, *Castle to Castle.*
Conversations with Professor Y.
London Bridge.

Normance.
North.
Rigadoon.
HUGO CHARTERIS, *The Tide Is Right.*
JEROME CHARYN, *The Tar Baby.*
ERIC CHEVILLARD, *Demolishing Nisard.*
MARC CHOLODENKO, *Mordechai Schamz.*
JOSHUA COHEN, *Witz.*
EMILY HOLMES COLEMAN, *The Shutter of Snow.*
ROBERT COOVER, *A Night at the Movies.*
STANLEY CRAWFORD, *Log of the S.S. The Mrs Unguentine.*
Some Instructions to My Wife.
ROBERT CREELEY, *Collected Prose.*
RENÉ CREVEL, *Putting My Foot in It.*
RALPH CUSACK, *Cadenza.*
SUSAN DAITCH, *L.C.*
Storytown.
NICHOLAS DELBANCO,
The Count of Concord.
Sherbrookes.
NIGEL DENNIS, *Cards of Identity.*
PETER DIMOCK, *A Short Rhetoric for Leaving the Family.*
ARIEL DORFMAN, *Konfidenz.*
COLEMAN DOWELL,
The Houses of Children.
Island People.
Too Much Flesh and Jabez.
ARKADII DRAGOMOSHCHENKO, *Dust.*
RIKKI DUCORNET, *The Complete Butcher's Tales.*
The Fountains of Neptune.
The Jade Cabinet.
The One Marvelous Thing.
Phosphor in Dreamland.
The Stain.
The Word "Desire."
WILLIAM EASTLAKE, *The Bamboo Bed.*
Castle Keep.
Lyric of the Circle Heart.
JEAN ECHENOZ, *Chopin's Move.*
STANLEY ELKIN, *A Bad Man.*
Boswell: A Modern Comedy.
Criers and Kibitzers, Kibitzers and Criers.
The Dick Gibson Show.
The Franchiser.
George Mills.
The Living End.
The MacGuffin.
The Magic Kingdom.
Mrs. Ted Bliss.
The Rabbi of Lud.
Van Gogh's Room at Arles.
FRANÇOIS EMMANUEL, *Invitation to a Voyage.*
ANNIE ERNAUX, *Cleaned Out.*
LAUREN FAIRBANKS, *Muzzle Thyself.*
Sister Carrie.
LESLIE A. FIEDLER, *Love and Death in the American Novel.*
JUAN FILLOY, *Op Oloop.*
GUSTAVE FLAUBERT, *Bouvard and Pécuchet.*
KASS FLEISHER, *Talking out of School.*
FORD MADOX FORD,
The March of Literature.
JON FOSSE, *Aliss at the Fire.*
Melancholy.
MAX FRISCH, *I'm Not Stiller.*

Man in the Holocene.
CARLOS FUENTES, Christopher Unborn.
Distant Relations.
Terra Nostra.
Where the Air Is Clear.
WILLIAM GADDIS, J R.
The Recognitions.
JANICE GALLOWAY, Foreign Parts.
The Trick Is to Keep Breathing.
WILLIAM H. GASS, Cartesian Sonata
and Other Novellas.
Finding a Form.
A Temple of Texts.
The Tunnel.
Willie Masters' Lonesome Wife.
GÉRARD GAVARRY, Hoppla! 1 2 3.
Making a Novel.
ETIENNE GILSON,
The Arts of the Beautiful.
Forms and Substances in the Arts.
C. S. GISCOMBE, Giscome Road.
Here.
Prairie Style.
DOUGLAS GLOVER, Bad News of the Heart.
The Enamoured Knight.
WITOLD GOMBROWICZ,
A Kind of Testament.
KAREN ELIZABETH GORDON,
The Red Shoes.
GEORGI GOSPODINOV, Natural Novel.
JUAN GOYTISOLO, Count Julian.
Exiled from Almost Everywhere.
Juan the Landless.
Makbara.
Marks of Identity.
PATRICK GRAINVILLE, The Cave of Heaven.
HENRY GREEN, Back.
Blindness.
Concluding.
Doting.
Nothing.
JACK GREEN, Fire the Bastards!
JIŘÍ GRUŠA, The Questionnaire.
GABRIEL GUDDING,
Rhode Island Notebook.
MELA HARTWIG, Am I a Redundant
Human Being?
JOHN HAWKES, The Passion Artist.
Whistlejacket.
ALEKSANDAR HEMON, ED.,
Best European Fiction.
AIDAN HIGGINS, A Bestiary.
Balcony of Europe.
Bornholm Night-Ferry.
Darkling Plain: Texts for the Air.
Flotsam and Jetsam.
Langrishe, Go Down.
Scenes from a Receding Past.
Windy Arbours.
KEIZO HINO, Isle of Dreams.
KAZUSHI HOSAKA, Plainsong.
ALDOUS HUXLEY, Antic Hay.
Crome Yellow.
Point Counter Point.
Those Barren Leaves.
Time Must Have a Stop.
NAOYUKI II, The Shadow of a Blue Cat.
MIKHAIL IOSSEL AND JEFF PARKER, EDS.,
Amerika: Russian Writers View the
United States.
DRAGO JANČAR, The Galley Slave.
GERT JONKE, The Distant Sound.

Geometric Regional Novel.
Homage to Czerny.
The System of Vienna.
JACQUES JOUET, Mountain R.
Savage.
Upstaged.
CHARLES JULIET, Conversations with
Samuel Beckett and Bram van
Velde.
MIEKO KANAI, The Word Book.
YORAM KANIUK, Life on Sandpaper.
HUGH KENNER, The Counterfeiters.
Flaubert, Joyce and Beckett:
The Stoic Comedians.
Joyce's Voices.
DANILO KIŠ, Garden, Ashes.
A Tomb for Boris Davidovich.
ANITA KONKKA, A Fool's Paradise.
GEORGE KONRÁD, The City Builder.
TADEUSZ KONWICKI, A Minor Apocalypse.
The Polish Complex.
MENIS KOUMANDAREAS, Koula.
ELAINE KRAF, The Princess of 72nd Street.
JIM KRUSOE, Iceland.
EWA KURYLUK, Century 21.
EMILIO LASCANO TEGUI, On Elegance
While Sleeping.
ERIC LAURRENT, Do Not Touch.
HERVÉ LE TELLIER, The Sextine Chapel.
A Thousand Pearls (for a Thousand
Pennies)
VIOLETTE LEDUC, La Bâtarde.
EDOUARD LEVÉ, Autoportrait.
Suicide.
SUZANNE JILL LEVINE, The Subversive
Scribe: Translating Latin
American Fiction.
DEBORAH LEVY, Billy and Girl.
Pillow Talk in Europe and Other
Places.
JOSÉ LEZAMA LIMA, Paradiso.
ROSA LIKSOM, Dark Paradise.
OSMAN LINS, Avalovara.
The Queen of the Prisons of Greece.
ALF MAC LOCHLAINN,
The Corpus in the Library.
Out of Focus.
RON LOEWINSOHN, Magnetic Field(s).
MINA LOY, Stories and Essays of Mina Loy.
BRIAN LYNCH, The Winner of Sorrow.
D. KEITH MANO, Take Five.
MICHELINE AHARONIAN MARCOM,
The Mirror in the Well.
BEN MARCUS,
The Age of Wire and String.
WALLACE MARKFIELD,
Teitlebaum's Window.
To an Early Grave.
DAVID MARKSON, Reader's Block.
Springer's Progress.
Wittgenstein's Mistress.
CAROLE MASO, AVA.
LADISLAV MATEJKA AND KRYSTYNA
POMORSKA, EDS.,
Readings in Russian Poetics:
Formalist and Structuralist Views.
HARRY MATHEWS,
The Case of the Persevering Maltese:
Collected Essays.
Cigarettes.
The Conversions.
The Human Country: New and

SELECTED DALKEY ARCHIVE PAPERBACKS

Martereau.
The Planetarium.
ARNO SCHMIDT, *Collected Novellas.*
Collected Stories.
Nobodaddy's Children.
Two Novels.
ASAF SCHURR, *Motti.*
CHRISTINE SCHUTT, *Nightwork.*
GAIL SCOTT, *My Paris.*
DAMION SEARLS, *What We Were Doing
and Where We Were Going.*
JUNE AKERS SEESE,
Is This What Other Women Feel Too?
What Waiting Really Means.
BERNARD SHARE, *Inish.*
Transit.
AURELIE SHEEHAN,
Jack Kerouac Is Pregnant.
VIKTOR SHKLOVSKY, *Bowstring.*
Knight's Move.
*A Sentimental Journey:
Memoirs 1917–1922.*
Energy of Delusion: A Book on Plot.
Literature and Cinematography.
Theory of Prose.
Third Factory.
Zoo, or Letters Not about Love.
CLAUDE SIMON, *The Invitation.*
PIERRE SINIAC, *The Collaborators.*
KJERSTI A. SKOMSVOLD, *The Faster I Walk,
the Smaller I Am.*
JOSEF ŠKVORECKÝ, *The Engineer of
Human Souls.*
GILBERT SORRENTINO,
Aberration of Starlight.
Blue Pastoral.
Crystal Vision.
*Imaginative Qualities of Actual
Things.*
Mulligan Stew.
Pack of Lies.
Red the Fiend.
The Sky Changes.
Something Said.
Splendide-Hôtel.
Steelwork.
Under the Shadow.
W. M. SPACKMAN,
The Complete Fiction.
ANDRZEJ STASIUK, *Dukla.*
Fado.
GERTRUDE STEIN,
Lucy Church Amiably.
The Making of Americans.
A Novel of Thank You.
LARS SVENDSEN, *A Philosophy of Evil.*
PIOTR SZEWC, *Annihilation.*
GONÇALO M. TAVARES, *Jerusalem.*
Joseph Walser's Machine.
*Learning to Pray in the Age of
Technique.*
LUCIAN DAN TEODOROVICI,
Our Circus Presents . . .
NIKANOR TERATOLOGEN, *Assisted Living.*
STEFAN THEMERSON, *Hobson's Island.*
The Mystery of the Sardine.
Tom Harris.
JOHN TOOMEY, *Sleepwalker.*
JEAN-PHILIPPE TOUSSAINT,
The Bathroom.
Camera.
Monsieur.

Running Away.
Self-Portrait Abroad.
Television.
The Truth about Marie.
DUMITRU TSEPENEAG,
Hotel Europa.
The Necessary Marriage.
Pigeon Post.
Vain Art of the Fugue.
ESTHER TUSQUETS, *Stranded.*
DUBRAVKA UGRESIC,
Lend Me Your Character.
Thank You for Not Reading.
MATI UNT, *Brecht at Night.*
Diary of a Blood Donor.
Things in the Night.
ÁLVARO URIBE AND OLIVIA SEARS, EDS.,
*Best of Contemporary Mexican
Fiction.*
ELOY URROZ, *Friction.*
The Obstacles.
LUISA VALENZUELA, *Dark Desires and
the Others.*
He Who Searches.
MARJA-LIISA VARTIO,
The Parson's Widow.
PAUL VERHAEGHEN, *Omega Minor.*
AGLAJA VETERANYI, *Why the Child Is
Cooking in the Polenta.*
BORIS VIAN, *Heartsnatcher.*
LLORENÇ VILLALONGA, *The Dolls' Room.*
ORNELA VORPSI, *The Country Where No
One Ever Dies.*
AUSTRYN WAINHOUSE, *Hedyphagetica.*
PAUL WEST,
Words for a Deaf Daughter & Gala.
CURTIS WHITE,
America's Magic Mountain.
The Idea of Home.
Memories of My Father Watching TV.
*Monstrous Possibility: An Invitation
to Literary Politics.*
Requiem.
DIANE WILLIAMS, *Excitability:
Selected Stories.*
Romancer Erector.
DOUGLAS WOOLF, *Wall to Wall.*
Ya! & John-Juan.
JAY WRIGHT, *Polynomials and Pollen.*
*The Presentable Art of Reading
Absence.*
PHILIP WYLIE, *Generation of Vipers.*
MARGUERITE YOUNG, *Angel in the Forest.*
Miss MacIntosh, My Darling.
REYOUNG, *Unbabbling.*
VLADO ŽABOT, *The Succubus.*
ZORAN ŽIVKOVIĆ, *Hidden Camera.*
LOUIS ZUKOFSKY, *Collected Fiction.*
VITOMIL ZUPAN, *Minuet for Guitar.*
SCOTT ZWIREN, *God Head.*

FOR A FULL LIST OF PUBLICATIONS, VISIT:
www.dalkeyarchive.com